IN MY MOTHER'S SHOES

Book 1 S.E. Jenkins Series

BUFFY DUMONT

I dedicate this book to my grandson, Carter, who continuously inspires me to be silly and to never forget my childlike spirit. His infectious smile and sense of humor leaves me wanting more, wanting to be better, and to always sing and dance in the rain.

Memere Loves you, Bon Homme.

<u>Chapter 1</u>

"Samantha Elizabeth!"

I froze- I'd been found.

Her voice, sharp and scary, caught me mid-action and my eyes followed her in the mirror until she appeared behind me.

I stood still and very quiet. Every inch of me, nervous. I swallowed hard. I could feel a lump forming in my throat.

I kept my eyes on myself, staring, in her antique oval mirror in her bedroom without breaking a gaze.

But, but I, I didn't go into THE ROOM that was off her side of the bedroom. Not this time. Not ever. I wasn't allowed; it was forbidden, and I wasn't *bothering* anyone! I thought to myself.

My voice was pinballed in my head, a scrambling panic because I was stuck.

In that moment. In her stare. Caught.

I mean, I was so sure she *was* supposed to be in the formal dining room playing cards with the Wednesday lady's group and those games almost *always* guaranteed me my own me-myself time. Time to pretend, time to be free, time to be who I am without anybody else watching my every move.

But not today, not this time.

This time she caught me, silly and pretending.

Pretending to be fancy, pretending to be posh and elite with my dripping six year old Southern accent.

She had caught me pretending to be *her*.

In my adventures that day, I found one of her gala dresses and was *only* trying it on, its grown-woman length was drowning my tiny child's body, my teeny toes lost in her size seven heels, hair peeled back tight to my skull in an unforgiving bun.

I'd done this before, many times, going undetected and putting everything back to right before she could see it but that day my luck ran plum out.

Because, this time, she caught me, and the worst was the horror on her face as she stood in the doorway looking in. I could feel her eyes piercing me, a look that was scary, but all too familiar. A look of disappointment that would be tattooed in my mind for a lifetime to come.

Her look would have sent anybody else in my first-grade class running for the corner of the room.

I had been in the middle of carefully applying her reddish pink lipstick around my tiny lips, pursed into a pucker, when she stopped me by barking out my full name.

Mother was the only one who called me by my full name.

"Samantha Elizabeth!" She snapped, eyebrow raised into her hairline as she forced me to meet her unrelenting gaze.

My heart was racing so hard I could feel it pulsing in the hollow of my throat. Almost floundering to breathe.

"Mother, I . . . I was only using your lipstick. It was. . ." I didn't know what to say; whatever I came up with wouldn't be enough, that I knew for sure.

I was, of course, forgetting that this was about much more than lipstick.

But, Mother, I thought to myself, *I felt pretty. I wanted to look like you on a special night out with Daddy. I wanted to feel, for just one minute, what it was like to be YOU."*

Quite honestly, I *didn't* know my mother.

I knew *of* her; her resume, her accomplishments, her peccadilloes.

Most of all, I knew what made her hair stand straight up about me, and could recite it like gospel.

I could recite it because she did so all the time.

Instead, I remained silent. To her, I was disobeying her rules, and that's all that mattered.

I stared straight down at the gown pooling around my feet, defeated.

She grabbed my chin, lifted it, and pulled my face close to hers until her lips were next to my ear, like she was someone she liked enough to share a secret with me.

I could barely hear her when she demanded in a whisper so the other ladies wouldn't hear, "You are doing it all *wrong*. "

She grabbed her handkerchief out of her sleeve and wet it with her mouth, then used it to wipe around my mouth, removing every careful stroke of red lipstick I applied, then snatched the lipstick tube out of my hand.

I knew what she was about to do.

"Samantha, don't you ever learn? It goes on like this!"

And, as she had many times before when correcting me, she re-applied the lipstick to my lips only this time as perfectly as she had her own, then she tilted my head back toward the mirror so I could see the difference between her work and mine.

As her cold fingers filled my chubby cheeks with heat, I took in her results, the look of accomplishment and triumph in her eyes.

She pivoted to the door, smiling, turned back and said, "Remember Samantha, stay out of my office."

Her office, forever known as THE ROOM, the only place in the house I was never truly welcomed to be in or allowed to go, was a room off Mother and Daddy's bedroom, always off-limits, always locked.

One day, I would find a way to get into that room.

And when I did . . .

"Sammy! SAM! Earth to Sam! Little lady, yoohoo!"

I was suddenly aware of Dexter snapping me back into place, back to reality, snatching me back from a memory that felt like yesterday but was over twenty years ago.

"Sammy Girl," Dexter said as his fingers snapped to hurry me along, "we have exactly a half an hour until cross examinations begin. You have got to wake up and quit daydreaming, because, sister, I'm not walking into court with an attorney who has her head in the clouds. Now, get out of those sweats, and make it happen." And snaps one last snap in the air.

There he goes again, bringing me back to the present day, keeping me grounded.

Dexter, my paralegal, therapist, outfit coordinator, and friend with a commitment to tell it like it is, is one of the few I can rely on.

I love my Dexter.

Probably the only person who has seen me in my raggedy converse, old comfy sweats that should never see the light of day, and hair that is thrown up in a messy bun. more than he has seen me in a pantsuit. Dexter knows how to listen to me, what I say and what I don't say. He reads between the lines with everyone he meets. Especially me.

Dexter is a good man.

I tell everyone who will listen that I would never want to practice law without him; he is my secret weapon.

But above all else, he just gets me, knows me better than anyone else.

He is also the only person alive that knows my secret.

"Thanks Dex, I was just thinking about . . . her," I tell him.

"You think I don't know that?" He snaps, shaking his head, exasperated with his one hand on his hip, waving his clipboard that he brings everywhere he goes for emphasis.

I swear this man acts like my keeper; he's lucky I love him.

Flapping his hands like he's herding a flock of chickens he says, "Let's get on with it!" as he shoves a soda in my hand like he's bribing a child to do their homework.

 "We have exactly thirty minutes, work your magic," he says and walks away with a stack of files and a load of sass humming something that sounds vaguely like 'Spoonful of Sugar' from Mary Poppins.

And there you have it.

That's Dexter.

I knew right away when I interviewed him that he was the one.

I interviewed a lot of applicants, some full of smoke and flattery, and some who were so unqualified and unconfident it's a wonder they could even introduce themselves when they sat down to talk to me.

So *painful*.

Then came Dexter.

I walked out to the waiting room expecting another uptight paralegal and there he was, sitting with his leg crossed over the other in his purple J. Crew Shirt and plaid bowtie, with matching socks bearing his terrier's face on them.

Everything in the office suddenly came to life around him, including me.

That was three years ago.

In fact, since I graduated law school and passed the bar, Dexter, in that little time has gotten to know me far better than anybody, even my own parents, despite having known me my entire life.

They know nothing about me. They don't know I am addicted to lemonheads candies, have an absurd collection of chapsticks in every location I'm in, have every picture license I have ever taken (is this hoarding? Ask Dexter to monitor), have a lifelong bucket list dream of going to the Louvre in Paris, and have a very strong dislike for corporate life, big houses, fancy cars, and.... practicing law.

Go figure.

What they don't know can't hurt them.

What they *do* know about me or *need* to know is that I was an easy child to raise, seldom having to be spoken to, and was never in trouble and that I am their only child that made them proud by achieving, doing, making something of myself. Achieving their checklist of me and never my own.

I was never boy-crazy, either, and am not much of a dating person, even now. This is why my mom feels the need to set me up constantly on blind dates with sons of her girlfriends from the city and, to boot, my mother brags to those same old ladies on my "healthy" income.

I *am* a successful attorney with a firm in the heart of Manhattan, set to make partner after just three short years, making a damn good living on my own terms.

Everything they know about my life is the bare minimum to keep them in a bragging zone giving them rights to share all of this success about me and what I'm doing.

Nothing more, nothing less.

Chapter 2

``NICE WORK, SAMMY!" Dexter has always loved my inner lion that comes out when I step inside the courtroom.

It's always so comical for him to watch me come out of my shell and win a case.

My competitive nature has placed me on the local legal system's radar and what nabbed me a partner position with the firm shortly after my internship ended.

"Thank you, Dex. What are you up to tonight?" I changed the subject because compliments make me so uneasy, I just don't know how to gracefully accept them.

"Well, you tell me Sam! Need I remind you that you have a show tonight at the gallery? I cleared my evening and am primed to attend! I make an oath to find out who keeps purchasing your paintings! Praying it's a tall, blonde, and handsome hottie!"

I roll my eyes but don't say anything.

I've told him over and over I don't care who it is; it could be the Pope for all the interest I had.

It wasn't my idea to even get involved in the Gallery until Dexter bet me that I could sell one of my paintings for at least two thousand dollars.

He won.

And I haven't stopped giving them paintings ever since.

Honestly, it could be anyone but I work under a pen name so they wouldn't know me, and I wasn't worried.

"Listen, Sam, I am determined to figure this out and you know it!" Dexter shoots me a grin, knowing that I love my secret life. It feels safe and cozy, But cocooned with invisible "do not disturb" signs all over it.

It didn't matter to me who bought them.

What mattered was what I was painting.

"I would Love to see you tonight," I continued, "Please, please bring Rich along! You two have been dating for three months, it's time I meet him!"

I adore seeing Dexter happy.

In fact, I adore love, I'm a romantic at heart. Romance movies, novels, couples kissing on street corners, elderly couples holding hands. And now my Dex is among the coupled up and happy. He is just so adorable about this Rich.

Since they started dating, Dexter now sings his way around the office every morning, the flowers Rich sends him fill our shared space with happiness, vibrancy, and life.

I have yet to experience this for myself.

My mom on the other hand, she can't wait to plan the wedding of a lifetime to show off her taste, her style, and her daughter dressed to the nines, but I have yet to find chemistry with her tragic set ups.

"Have supper with us before the showing?" Dexter asks, "You're right, it's time you two meet. Come to the apartment and let's celebrate the evening with dinner and wine. I can't wait to see your new painting!"

I *love* the way Dexter gets excited about my work.

My biggest, and maybe, only, fan.

"I would love to, but I haven't heard from my mother in days. Something is up. I really must stop by the house and check in."

Mom calls me constantly.

She doesn't go a day without snooping for information about my personal life, a private life that doesn't exist.

I'm always well prepared for the phone calls, but her recent silence *was* concerning to me.

The only time she ever went this long without calling was the time I walked out of a date she had set me up on and trust me, she was so upset that she didn't speak to me for a few days.

Mom's friend, Camilla, recommended a date with her "darling son" when he came to the city from upstate New York. He was just a "darling" when he forced himself on me in the middle of a movie, trying to kiss me and his octopus' hands were all over me, everywhere except in his popcorn bowl or in his own space. We were one hour into the date and next thing I knew I drew back, punched him in the face, and left the movie theater.

Mom went days without calling me.

I knew she was mad and embarrassed and I may have overreacted, but I needed peace with my mother.

I knew what to do to move us past it.

I called Camilla's son to check up on the fat lip I gave him, and he fell all over himself apologizing to me.

I'm certain his mother, too, gave him the same silent treatment mine was giving me- neither of us was showing the best behavior and it was a bad look.

Regardless, Mom was pleased with my effort and life went on.

So you see, dating has never been for me.

I repeat. Never been for me.

I am not good at it. I'm awkward. A bad dater.

If you think about it, it brings way too much stress and anxiety for something that's supposed to be fun, so I avoid it at all costs.

Too much to think about, dating, the pressure of it, and the very real possibility of it not working out.

The anticipation before the ask, will he or won't he. Should I ask *him*?

The whole getting ready thing. Makeup or no makeup? What do I wear? Too many decisions to be made.

They should offer classes for this kind of stuff; I would totally take it.

Then, I could see who else sucks at it and maybe date them and then, voila! Problem solved, hopefully for life.

Dexter interrupts my thoughts.

"Alright, then. Check up on your mama and let her tear you down and then come moping into the gallery like a freshly scolded ten-year-old. Don't tell me that I didn't warn you!" He winks at me with a grin.

His cute little wink gets him a lot of free passes. Sassy boy.

I go to answer him and realize I don't have any fight left in me today, not even a good-natured one.

Dexter's right, she has a way of tearing my self-esteem apart; reminding me that living alone can only lead me to the life of an old maid, the same old tired things every time.

But as much as mother is stone cold at times, she has a good heart, and not hearing from her is unusual when nothing crazy has happened.

Usually, when mom wants to do something kind for me, she sends my dad to the office to take me to lunch or has him drop off a homemade lunch that she apparently had "nothing" to do with. However, only mom knew that chicken salad sandwiches without lettuce on cold white bread are my favorite, and she always draws a heart on the sandwich bag with my name in the middle, even now that I'm an adult.

Mom knows what I like, she just never takes credit for it.

She really does care, though. I know this.

I'm still holding out hope for her heart to shine one of these days for all the world to see as much as I am that I, one day, see what part of her is in me.

She struggles with affection, and she always has, but Mom has always found a way to show me she loves me.

But recently with no visits from dad? No lovingly packed lunches? No call?

Something is up and I am popping for a surprise visit to find out what it is.

I stop by my place to grab my outfit for the night because half the gallery won't recognize me in my three-piece suit and that's part of what I love about the gallery's visitors. I can peel back my mask and be the real me, raw and vulnerable, and they still accept me for who I am.

For now, it was time to check on the parents. I needed to. I was their only child.

I always have been, and always will be, intimidated by rolling up the driveway of my parents' house.

The entrance of the house included tall steel gates edged with rose bushes along the front of the home on all sides and edges of the property.

You must either talk to my parents through the speaker at the gate or know the code for the keypad and mom, forever concerned someone will break in and rob them blind, changes it constantly.

Luckily, she isn't great at coming up with new codes; it's always the year I was born, or the month and year combined.

After a couple of tries the gates slowly opened.

Those gates.

It cracks me up every time I come home to visit because those gates are a perfect representation of my mother; cold, steel gates that take way too much time to open, closed at will, and then there is no way of getting in. I know my mom, she loves the drama of the doors opening slowly, as if we were entering Buckingham Palace. Oh mother- the drama!

*   *   *   *   *
  *   *   *   *

"Hello? Anyone home?" I yell nice and loud as I open the front door, not because I thought she might be all the way on the third floor but because, since I was a child, I'm tickled by the way it echoes.

"Samantha, is that you?" I hear daddy's tiny voice answering from way inside the house, maybe the back patio area where we eat breakfast when the weather is nice.

I walk down the hall past the living room, through the kitchen, and into where I loved spending time with him every morning before he took me to school as a child.

I walk in to find dad with his head in his hands, elbows resting on the table; he lifts his gaze when he hears me approach and I can instantly tell something is very, very wrong because my dad, my rock, is crying.

I know my dad like the back of my hand, I have spent my life studying his every move, his every glance. I just *adore* my dad.

He was a professor at a nearby community college and many times, as a child, I spent afternoons in his lectures, watching him teach, because mom was busy shopping in the city or volunteering.

I preferred being with daddy. He called me his buddy and I *loved* that nickname; I always preferred being dad's buddy over mom's prim and proper young lady.

When he took me to work with him, I would sneak out when he wasn't looking for a peek at the art department, with the most beautiful art right in front of me, close enough to touch.

I would climb the stairs to the balcony, look down at the students while they worked and stare at every stroke of the brush as it brought their paintings to life. The students each had their own canvas and pallet, and I spent hours imagining life as an artist.

It became my lifelong dream- it also became my obsession.

"Daddy? Are you okay?" I rush over to where he's sitting, "Are you hurt?"

He says nothing, he only cries harder. I wrap my arms around holding him close to me and the comfort makes him sob.

What in the world was going on!!

"Oh Samantha, your mom…" He looks up, his eyes tired, and red.

Oh gosh, what has happened? I feel myself begin to panic.

"*Dad*?" I kneel to his level and hold his face in my hands, "Where is mom?"

He can't bring himself to speak words so I leave him at the table and begin shouting for mom, going room to room to room in a full, frenzied panic.

"Mom. Mom???? Mom!!!!!! Are you here? Mom, where are you?" I can feel my dad following me.

"Samantha no, no, no please no please stop, your mother is finally resting. Please don't wake her," He begs as he catches up to me.

"Dad, so help me god, if you don't tell me what's going on . . ."

"Samantha, honey sit down," He gently places his hand on my arm and guides me to the kitchen table where I was the only child allowed to sit, the table that held so many adult conversations and just me, alone, during holidays and parties.

It was also the table that helped me learn how to become invisible.

"A couple of weeks ago, your mom had her physical. She told the doctor she was experiencing severe lower back pain and must have been sleeping all wrong. You know your mother. She reads before bed and always stays awake later than I ever could and sometimes falls asleep sitting up. We just thought it was that. We thought she was just sore. She told me it was nothing for me to worry about, Sammy"

"Dad, for God's sake get to the point." I am losing my mind, my patience, and shortly, my shit.

"Samantha, stop, please let me finish," Dad begs, voice calm.

"They took her blood to see her liver function, then scheduled a cat scan, and that's when they found a mass. Samantha . . ." he trails off, unable to hold back more tears.

I have never seen my father cry before except when we watched the movie *Miss Saigon* together.

My sweet father, my gentle, sweet father just can't continue to speak and begins to sob almost like the flooded gates have been opened.

Then he, too, begins to talk, quick and panicky, "Samantha, she has had so many appointments and is scheduled for surgery a week from now, they didn't make her wait, they didn't think it wise. They are certain it's cancer, it's just determining the treatment plan after. Sammy, courses start soon, and I have to work. I have no idea what we are going to do . . ." He tries to continue but I can't hear anymore. He needs someone to take over.

Well, this leaves me or the siblings I begged for years to have.

"Dad, Dad, sshhh shhhh Daddy listen to me" I held his hands together under mine and as gentle and as calm as I could say, I said, "tell me what you need me to do, Dad. I'm here."

"Samantha, if it's already stage three like they think… it's in her lymph nodes. She's sick, Samantha, she's sick and will need chemo and radiation. She will need rides to the hospital, and will need help to get in and out of bed. Sam, I don't know how I can be in two places. I could ask for a semester off, I have a lot of sick time accrued, but Sammy the math department is already short staffed, and this is happening so fast. We have to go back to the hospital tomorrow morning for pre-testing before the surgery."

I know I need to be strong. My "get-it-done" lawyer side kicks in and I say, "Daddy. SHHH. Stop. I am *here*. I can help, I can take her. We can take turns. I can help every single day. Dexter is at the office and will send my files to my laptop at the hospital. Dad, I'm flexible. I can work remotely right from Mom's room. You have school starting next week, and I can do this, dad. But dad, first . . . have you gotten a second opinion?"

I cannot bel*ie*ve he is telling me this a week before she goes in. What on earth are they thinking? How did it get to this? How much have they been dealing with for weeks, without me? Am I *that* checked out?

I want to cry, fall to my knees, and apologize for all the awful things I have said, thought and told others about my mother.

I want to beg for forgiveness for things they don't even know I've done.

But Dad needs me, and this is what I do best.

I handle things, and I win.

I make dad a cup of hot tea and pull out my open bag of peanut M&Ms from my bag and place them in front of him. He takes a sip of the tea, and then he sees the peanut M&M's and I get a small, gentle smile. Our secret snack together.

Sugar was always out of the question at home, so it became our afternoon secret snack when I was little on our way back home from work.

I was his girl, and his girl was going to fix this.

And I need to see my mom.

I walk to mom's room and find the door open a bit.

I can smell her scent as I quietly tiptoe into her room, the fragrance that has always been hers, the smell of hothouse gardenias.

It was a smell that will soon, no doubt, long for like nothing else.

"Mother", I whisper but there's no response, she's out like a light, her eyelids sealed against the outside world in rest.

I walk over to where she's laying flat on the bed with a blanket tucked around her.

She looks peaceful, almost healthy.

She almost looks . . . kind.

I shake my head, clearing the thought away and see that her office door is open.

This room has never been opened, I think, curious and curiouser.

I barely take a step towards the office when she catches my arm with her hand, nimble like Bruce Lee.

"Samantha," She speaks but doesn't open her eyes, "Samantha, can you make sure the ladies do not learn of this? Can you make certain your father is able to attend his racquetball class tomorrow?"

I kneel bedside with my hand holding hers, "Mother, I'm here, we'll get through this together. Dad and I spoke, I know everything and it will all be ok. Mom, you are so strong."

Eyes still closed, she smirks, "I'm tired Samantha. Be a good young lady and as I asked, while I rest."

I think to myself, That's It mother? Really? That's all I get? Your rules, as usual, even now. Your rules? Fine. Rest. Rest while I hold everything together around you.

Then I feel the vibration of my cell phone ring.

I look at my watch and realize I'm late for the gallery.

Shit!

I slide my hand from hers and say, "Ok, Mother, I will be back tomorrow, I promise. I'll go to the hospital with you."

I look back at her one last time as I step out of the room and catch her opening her eyes to peek at me.

She sees me looking at her and quickly closes her eyes again but says nothing.

That woman. That stubborn, stubborn woman.

"May the stubbornness help her heal", I mumble to myself as I grab my jacket and head back to the kitchen where Dad is already on the phone.

I can tell he's speaking to a colleague by his tone of voice.

He covers the receiver and says "Samantha, I'll call you later. I love you."

I nod, "I love you too Daddy. So much." and I kiss him on his forehead.

I walk out to my car and my mind reels, even as I drive past the gates.

What the hell just happened, I think.

I know I need to pull it together.

I'm about to walk into a room full of people at the gallery and need my game face on when people ask questions about my work.

I will wrap my brain around everything else later, on my own timeline, because I truly just don't know how to feel.

Or if I feel anything.

Mother has always commanded our home, our lives, and now she needs us to be the ones in control, handling everything.

Weirdly, this is the most foreign concept to me right now, maybe even more-so than her being seriously, direly ill.

Her being out of control is just so damned foreign.

__Chapter 3__

"Inhale, exhale," I say to myself, "exhale, inhale . . ."

Honestly, at this moment I do not want to exhale.

I just want to stop time, slow it all down.

"I was just going to visit my parents to check in. Never in my wildest dreams did I expect this. My strong, invincible, hard-nosed mother and my sweet father that is so calm, so passive. And now my entire family is literally upside down. How is this happening right now?" I say to myself and then shake my head in disbelief, trying to shrug it off but know full well, I can't.

On the other hand, there is no reason why Dad and I can't work together to get her to treatment, and I can work virtually when needed. Dexter always has the office under control, and he never panics, he can handle anything thrown his way while I help them.

I can help her; I can be Dad's strength.

I can do this.

Handling the "unhandle-able" is what I do.

I pop Billy Joel's greatest hits into the cassette of my '76 Beetle and drive to a song that I would normally sing along to at the top of my lungs, windows down, carefree, on my way to the next thing.

But today 'My Life" isn't fitting the bill.

I fast forward to 'New York State of Mind' and try that instead.

This, for some reason, is when it all lands.

Hard.

I feel the blood rushing from head to toe, hard and fast.

I am about to spend weeks on end with my mother and I have to make the most of that time while I prepare myself for the worst.

I shake my head, snapping myself into go mode, then throw the bug into gear and get my butt to the gallery as fast as I can.

The next few hours are surreal.

My brain is at a standstill.

People at the gallery swirl by me, champagne flutes in hand, pausing to gaze at the paintings that are hanging wall to wall.

There's soft classical music playing in the background, and I hear the blend of conversations, about paintings and their prices.

I'm only there in the gallery tonight in body, not in spirit.

I'm too numb.

How is this happening?

If I hadn't gone to check in, would my parents have even told me?

Why did it take me so long to get concerned when I didn't hear from them?

My thoughts are in a nonstop, persistent spiral that I cannot stop, no matter how hard I try; I can't even grab onto one long enough to focus.

WAIT! And it hits me

I do have a client who works for Mount Sinai- I can easily get in touch with them in the morning.

He has always been so grateful for my help, maybe he can refer mom to someone who will give her the best care, a fighting chance!! It is only fifteen minutes from my condo and the morning commute would be so easy.

I can run to mom's, grab her, and go.

This *will* work!!

"Jenkins!" Dexter blurts when he sees me, snapping me out of my thoughts so abruptly I'm startled beyond belief.

"Dexter! Do NOT jump me," I bark at him.

He recoils, stunned by my stinging tone, then pauses, one eyebrow up, his lips curling into a snarl as he steps back.

"Um, OK. I guess this is *not* the time to introduce you to the person who just purchased your painting for five grand." He turns from me and walks away.

Damn it.

I take a deep breath, tuck my hair behind my ears, apply a fresh layer of ChapStick and spot someone standing in front of my painting.

I'm not in the mood, but I need to thank the buyer.

Here goes nothing.

I walk over to the painting, slap my game face on and extend my hand politely out to the gentlemen gazing at my painting.

I'll be polite, thank him briefly for his interest in my work and his support, then leave.

I want to wrap this up and skedaddle, I am doing no good being here.

"Hi! I'm S.E. Jenkins; I wanted to introduce myself and thank you for your interest in my work."

I catch a strong scent of cologne in the air. It has me lifting my nose to the air wanting to see if it was him. Boy, he smells good.

Focus, Samantha! I swallow hard.

"It was inspired by Central Park's Conservatory Garden. Have you ever been? It holds the most beautiful gardens and I absolutely *love* the pink and white crab apple trees and how the colors remind me of a Monet painting when the sunlight hits it at the right time of the day. It feels majestic and almost alive. The sunlight on it looks like a staircase to heaven. I was there when I was a little girl, my dad and I would pass it and it was always something I would look forward to..."

There is no stopping me, I am talking nonstop.

One. nonstop. sentence.

Can't stop, won't stop.

This happens when I'm nervous.

Talk, talk, and neck gets red too, but only when I'm around men who . . .

Wait. Focus.

He smells good, yes, and his clear blue eyes . . .

But focus.

Breathe.

Ok. So, this is not going well so far, and I just need to breathe.

Once I stop talking, the guy looks at me, almost cocking his head to one side which, may I add, causes his hair to fall slightly over his left eye.

I snap back to reality when he gives me an egotistical, snarky smirk and says, "You must have me mistaken for someone else. I'm just looking."

Then he raises his glass of champagne aloft as though toasting me.

How rude. I collect myself and need to respond with something intelligent or at least not sound ridiculous, again.

"OH! OK, I'm sorry, they mentioned someone purchased this painting here and . . . you know what, never mind. Thank you for coming to the show this evening."

I pivot and walk away right out the front door into the cool air of the night feeling foolish.

Nope not tonight, I'm *not* doing this, I am done.

I'm going home.

*　　　　*　　　　*　　　　*　　　　*
　　*　　　　*　　　　*　　　　*

Walking into my condo on West 115th St has never felt so good.

I shut the door behind myself and slide down, melting into the floor of my doorway with my back sliding down the door.

Leroy comes running, meowing and probably thinking I'm about to feed him as this was our "norm", but I can't move.

Tears streaming down my face I try to brush him away and I say, "Leroy not right now."

He is purring so loud and rubbing feverishly against my legs that are tucked up into my chest.

"Leroy, what the hell happened today? What the hell am I going to do? How can I do this? And why, for shits sake, am I their only child!"

I sit, curled up in the front hallway by the door, for what seems like forever and I cry until I sob and I sob until I don't have any tears left.

Damn those good cries that feel so good. I feel like my heart has been ripped right out of my chest.

Duty calls with Leroy keeps reminding me that he's hungry, so I get up, pull my sweater off, toss it on the couch, and head for the kitchen.

After I feed him, I make sure he is good to go and pop open a soda, grab my pillow and blanket, and lay on the couch with some trash TV. I need to calm every part of me down and relax.

I need rest. I need my couch. Not my bed, just my couch.

My bed will remind me how alone I feel tonight even if tomorrow is a new day. A bed that has only had me as its only resident.

My brain starts to reflect on this day. When I woke up this morning I could have never predicted its fate. My brain starts to spiral until my thoughts land on that guy standing in front of my painting looking at me like I'm some kind of rambling bunny loving tree hugger, smirking like I'm a joke. I could totally tell he thought he was better than me, than most likely everyone there. What a jerk. If Dexter had saw and heard the way he was carrying on he would have told me "Girl, that one there is a Butter Heart Boy. Everything is delicious about him except his Heart."

I giggle thinking how Dexter would have come back at him with something witty. I shake my head, with disgust.

You know what, forget you and your Ralph Lauren baby blue shirt and your blue eyes and your smell that probably melts all your girlfriends.

But not me.

Not ever.

Nothing about you will ever melt me, buddy.

Chapter 4

I munch on cheese curls, my Walkman in hand and my Sony headphones wrapped around my head, my seven-year-old legs criss-cross applesauce where I sit in the balcony above the art classroom at the College Daddy teaches at.

My arms hang over the railing above my head as I peer down at the students painting behind their easels.

Directly in front of the class sits a mommy with a long white muslin sheet draped over her body and tucked under her arms is an itty-bitty baby.

Their skin is so pale and looks as soft as satin.

The mommy has the longest hair I have ever seen, and I wonder when I was that little if my mommy had long hair like that.

I bet my mommy would braid this mommy's hair, so it looked neat and out of her face.

My imagination begins to go wild.

I even bet this mommy has a voice as soft as a whisper; I bet her baby likes it.

I wonder if my she would be her friend.

Her baby is sleeping, and I wonder if she held me like that and if we looked that beautiful together.

I bet it was daddy that held me. I bet he held me a lot.

Mrs. Demeter is the professor for this class.

She always sits in the back watching her students concentrate and paint and always includes me in the class with little gestures like a wink at me when I watch them.

She can always feel me up on the balcony and has never once shooed me away.

She's nice to me.

I used my lined paper from my backpack to paint her once and it was fun.

My mommy packed my backpack for me with paper and crayons to keep me busy and I used them to pretend I was a student and listen to the instructions, then paint my own pictures.

My own little self-contained art class.

"Samantha, my class is over sweetie, are you ready to head out?" Daddy peers at me from the top of the staircase.

"Yes, Daddy," I whisper back and hold my finger to my lips so he knows we need to whisper. I took one last peek at the model, her baby and the portraits on the easels they were painting of her.

In this moment I could live here forever because I love it. I like how it feels.

I rip the page out and tuck it neatly, flat under the carpet with the rest of my pictures for safe keeping.

And we left, Daddy and I, together.

"Samantha," Daddy said as we walked down the sidewalk of campus holding hands, "let's get ice cream!"

Oh, he is so much fun!

He loves to surprise me, but I know that Mommy is probably home by now and everyone being on time is important to her.

"Daddy, it's almost dinner time." I reminded him.

"Samantha, today we will have dessert before dinner," he says and squeezes my hand, then continues with a trivia question.

I love it when daddy thinks I'm smart and asks me questions.

"Samantha, do you know what desserts spelled backwards is?"

Hmmm, I don't think I know this answer, but I know if daddy doesn't know either, he's relying on me to know.

"Um," I start to sound out the syllables.

I need to know this- I wonder why he doesn't? I bet it's because Mother doesn't let us eat sugar. That's why he doesn't know, he needs more sugar.

Me too, then.

I thought about it more and finally said, "Daddy, I think I need to wait to tell you, cause I need to ask my teacher at school tomorrow. She knows a lot, Daddy. She even knows that Jimmy at school can't eat peanuts cause if he does then he will need to go to the office cause he needs a shot to stay alive," I ramble on as though I am teaching my father something big.

Daddy grins, "Well, Samantha, today is your lucky day. Dessert spelled backwards spells stressed and every time you feel stressed it's very important to eat something yummy and filled with sugar," he explained.

Wow! Every time?!

I wonder if it would be ok with mommy if we did, or maybe this was another one of those times that it's just between me and daddy.

I like those times.

Times just between me and my daddy were safe for me to giggle the loudest, to chew gum with my mouth open, and to draw pictures of little puppies and pretty flowers.

'Ok daddy," I finally said, "I am stressed."

I giggle when his eyes widen comically.

"Samantha, me too! Let's share a hot fudge sundae!" He says, swinging our hands back and forth between us.

I love my daddy.

He is handsome and silly and smart.

He lets me walk through puddles and lets me give my sandwich to people on the subway who have dirty hands and are sitting on the ground.

He lets me ride in the car with the windows down, my hair crazy in the wind.

This time we sit together at a booth with our long spoons and the same waitress from last week waits on us.

"Well, look who came to visit me today! Professor Jenkins and Sammy!" She calls over to us and winks at me.

"Hi Cindy," I greet her and wave, "we're stressed."

"Oh really?" she giggles looking over at Daddy and says, "I'm going to take care of that for you, then. How about your usual?" She looks at daddy for his approval.

"Of course! Because Sammy here had a hard day at college. She spent her afternoon in class and needs a break," dad tells her.

I beam at him- I bet he is proud of me, but I wonder if she knows I don't go to school where daddy works.

Today, we will pretend and today I'm an artist.

Cindy returns with our ice cream, and we eat it as fast as she dropped it on the table.

"Sam, what do you want to be when you grow up?" Daddy asks.

Looking at daddy, he looks like a teacher with his big glasses and fancy shirts with buttons he wears to school. I want to look fancy too, like him. I bet fancy people make a lot of money and if I make a lot of money, I can go to Mrs. Demeter's art class and sit down on the floor with the other students and paint.

"Daddy, I think I need to make a lot of money. I want a fun bedroom with a bunk bed instead of my canopy bed. I also want to have one of those blankets with different colored squares instead of the puffy one I have." I start to get excited because it's so much fun to talk about being a grown up.

"And I want one of the giant easels in my room and daddy I want to be able to eat in my room, too!"

Sometimes, I talk nonstop and lightning fast when I get excited.

Daddy is smiling and then it turns into a giggle, and he reaches across the table and grabs my hands and says, "Sammy, whatever you want to be, I will always love you and always believe in you."

"But Daddy, what do you and mommy think would be a good job for me?"

I knew mommy wouldn't approve of my bunk beds and making her happy was the right thing because when I did, she would smile and sometimes hold my hand.

Daddy's face changes.

"Well, Sammy, your mother would love for you to be happy and would love for you to have a job that makes you happy. Your mother studied law in college, and I bet she would LOVE to see you be a judge one day."

And there you have it.

That's what I would do, become a judge.

Mother would be so happy, and daddy would be too.

A judge I would be.

I would be a judge and I would be able to judge . . .

*   *   *   *   *
       *   *   *   *

"Objection your honor, the defendant has already testified that she observed the vehicle passing her home, not that she observed *who* was driving it. Her reference to my client's vehicle has not been placed in evidence."
I'm certain we have this case, but this Judge is also difficult.

How this particular judge landed herself a seat in this courtroom is beyond me, but it's a job I never want.

Mother wants me sitting there with the title, but I do not.

"Good Work Samantha," Dexter is waiting outside the courtroom for me, ready to jump back into business.

But I notice he hasn't made eye contact all morning. I know we have to talk, and I needed to apologize for my behavior at the gallery.

He's always there to support me and not only was I rude last night, but I also bolted with no explanation and no goodbye.

"Dexter, we have to talk."

He was silent.

"Dex, I can explain about last night. I left the gallery because I had an insane and kind of terrible evening, and- "

Dexter takes a deep breath, holds it, then blows it out loud and noisily and the sound halts me. I can tell he is processing and filtering his thoughts, separating me being his boss from being his best friend.

"Sam, there is no reason to explain. Your mother came this morning. She said she was on her way to an appointment and thought you were going to go. She ended up explaining what was going on and that's why I'm here. I canceled your 3pm and I rescheduled your 9am tomorrow. Go be with her, Sammy. The ice queen is melting, and she needs you."

Chapter 5

I don't know when, exactly, mom started correcting me or, rather, I am not sure when she realized I wasn't perfect and needed constant correction.

Regardless of when it started, it's a habit of hers and I know the weeks to come are about to rock my world.

But now we are here, at the doctor's office, the three of us waiting to have a conversation that I could have never predicted a month ago. How we ended up here, I still can't wrap my mind around.

The Medical Assistant in her scrubs calls us in, and we file into a tiny little office.

Dr. Piper, Mom's doc, offers me a stool because both patient chairs across from his desk are taken.

Yup, give me the stool. I'm the pinch hitter for this team, anyway, I want to say.

I can feel my mother's eyes on me, almost like she can read my mind and she gives me her famous behave-yourself-two-count-bug-eyed look.

"Ok, folks, thank you for coming in on such short notice."

"Thank you for calling us right away with the results, we are very eager to establish a plan for Eleanors care," Dad politely responded.

The doctor gives him a nod and then turns to Mother.

"So to recap; Eleanor, you came in with chronic lower back pain starting in your abdomen, an area of the body typically associated with the pancreas, which is why we ordered CAT scans and an MRI to explore further. The antigen results of the blood work show. . ."

I can't take this and interrupt, loudly clearing my throat.

"Excuse me, doctor," I say, cutting off this long gust of wind for a Doctor, at the knees, "Can you, please, skip to the results? Could we discuss this? My mom has been through a lot leading up to this moment and we need to know what we're facing. Can you just give us your findings?"

I look over at my dad and can see he's deeply relieved I spoke up.

Mom, on the other hand, reaches over and squeezes my hand firmly as she politely turns to the doctor and says, "Please excuse my daughter. She is a VERY Successful attorney and is used to being in charge. Please continue."

The doctor clears his throat, as well, and goes forward.

"As I was saying. Eleanor, the tests we ran show that you have pancreatic cancer."

The room falls silent.

He pauses, a pause allowing us to jump in with any questions we might have.

But not us, not the Jenkins family.

The Jenkins were taught to compose ourselves, always; to process first and react later.

We don't even know where we are, if this is real, and none of us can, or want to, believe it.

I grab my notebook and pen, am poised to ask a question, but he continues speaking.

"Pancreatic Adenocarcinoma is what you have. Because of the location of the cells, we would like to schedule you for surgery immediately to remove the mass and dive directly into your post-op care and treatment plan. Please understand it will only be during the exploratory portion of the surgery that I can assess what portion of the cancer can or cannot be removed. Dr. Hayden Bryant, a newer addition to our team, will assist; he has a great deal of experience with this specific type of cancer. With Dr. Bryant's involvement, I am confident we will come to a clear diagnosis and definitive treatment plan."

He takes an unnecessarily loud and distracting breath, then addresses me and my father.

"I know this is a lot for all of you to take in. Eleanor will need a lot of daily help and care as, after surgery and during treatment, she will be able to do very little. Is there anyone available to help in the next few weeks?"

The room plunges into an awkward silence as both my parents pin me with their eyes.

My brain is screaming inside my head, demanding to know how this is happening, insisting that I bolt, NOW.

How can this be happening? My life was trucking along so smoothly- no one was getting hurt, no one was complaining.

I was working long days and enjoying my nights, living my quiet little life on my terms. I am even thinking going back to life with Mother running our lives is far better than this.

I think for a moment.

This old, bald man with halitosis is telling me that I need to dedicate all my time and energy to caring for my mother who has always struggled with caring for me?

I finally, slowly raise my hand like I'm being called on in a classroom.

"Me . . . I will be the one . . . helping . . . my . . . mother . . ." I share.

I' m not sure if it's goosebumps or chills that crawl up my back, but I am confident it's happening because life is about to get real.

Either real hard or real comical, or both.

"Wonderful!" he says and stands as he closes the chart with a snap.

"My office assistant will be speaking with you all, on your way out, to go over all the details of your pre op and schedule it on a day that works for you. I'd like to schedule the surgery within the next week; that way we can have a better handle on what's needed for the best preventative care possible." He says and then he exits the room.

JUST. Like. That.

I scoop up the stool and place it back in the corner, then head for the door with my parents directly behind me.

I stop short and pause to look behind me; when I do, I catch my mother taking the same exact stool that I placed in the corner and see her move it more to the left, a few absolutely pointless inches off from where I set it.

This is classic.

Correcting me is what she loves most to do.

We meet with the assistant and spend the next hour going over paperwork, insurance coverage, dates to schedule, additional bloodwork and after post-op care appointments.

Thankfully, I have my laptop and immediately begin punching in dates and times and catalogue what needs to be done for mom right now.

I move into administrative mode and begin to prepare my mind, my time and my life around the next few weeks, maybe even months.

I know one thing; I will need Dexter NOW more than ever!

I'm heading into a part of my life that would prove to be unforgettable in the most terrible way.

Chapter 6

If anyone ever tells you *not* to google an illness, believe them.

It's been days since I sat, took a pause, and a moment to collect my thoughts let alone my feelings so being back at my place, after this long day with my parents, feels very overdue.

But the sound of silence is unsettling when you can't quiet your racing, frantic mind.

I dial Dexter's number; I know it's a long shot that he's awake, but I need a pick-me-up fix of Dexter's fun personality.

The phone rings five times and just when I expect his voice mail I hear his sleepy voice on the line, mumbling, "Hey Sam."

"Dex, I'm sorry for calling so late but I just needed to hear your voice. I'm so sorry."

"Quit apologizing, Sammy. I'm here, talk to me." I hear him sit up in bed. He is so good; I love him so much. He is a safe place for me to land, a true best friend.

Not sure how I would work at the firm without him- not sure I would want to.

"I don't even know where to begin," I pause, then, "Something feels so cold about mom having pancreatic cancer. It's like it hasn't hit any of us yet. Dex, she is acting so cold, hard to read and honestly not even focused at all on this. She acts like nothing is going on."

Dexter interrupts and asks, "okayyyyy, well, what about your father? And you?"

"Dad is quiet, and sad, and I'm just there. Just following along at appointments, taking notes. I guess I'm really not sure what to do. She is… I guess It's still the Eleanor show, but not in the right way. Shit, I don't know. I just know she's acting like nothing is happening." I blurt in one long stream.

"Look. We know her. We know how she deals. We know she's always in charge. We also know when to leave her alone and let it simmer. Sam, it's a lot for her, and as cold as the old bag can be, it will hit her. Maybe at ninety miles an hour but it will start settling in. Just buckle up, Sam. Prepare yourself. Because I have a stinging feeling this will be rough."

He's right, I know this. I also know I need to take charge without making her feel like she's lost control.

I need to be present and keep my head together.

It would be so much easier if I had a sibling to help me.

"Yeah, I know. Just please keep feeding me work to do, I will have my computer with me all the time. Sometimes I may not have service but PLEASE send me anything to keep me occupied. And DON'T forget to water Esmeralda, Dexter. My mom will wring my neck if I let the plant she gave me die!"

He giggles because Esmeralda and I go way back, she gave me this plant on my first day of work, and it's a constant question from her if I've managed to kill my plant yet. Always determined to keep it alive but always needing reminders from Dexter to water it.

"Do *not* worry girl, I got this! Hey, I wanted to tell you before I forget, Sam, to bring your sketch pad along when you take your mom to appointments. Hospitals are great for people watching. I think this will help you in your downtime."

I can't with this one, he is so good.

"Thank you. And I'm so sorry I woke you up. Love you, Dex!"

"Ditto, Sammy. We'll talk tomorrow. Get some rest girl!" He says and hangs up.

I pause, take a deep breath, and close my eyes.

At this moment, I feel loved. I feel needed and like I belong to someone, even just in friendship.

I get up from the couch and slip my jammies on. I'm not tired and need to do something. All I've done today since leaving the hospital with my parents is Google pancreatic cancer.

My advice?

Don't google this.

Just don't.

Per the internet, we should jump straight to choosing a funeral home, which is ridiculous because computer technology has not met Mrs. Eleanor Smith-Jenkins.

So, I do what I always do when my mind is a four-lane highway; I grab my paint brushes from the corner, unwrap my new canvases, and set them up near the open window looking over the city.

This is always my answer, always what silences every kind of stress and pulls out a part of me where I feel my best. Painting to me is like a violinist in the middle of a stage, eyes closed, body moving to the sound of each finger creating a note every time a string is touched.

When I paint, I somehow create music in my heart.

Each color comes to life like a musical note. It carefully pulls the raw emotions that I struggle to feel, twists them in every direction and places them gently back into my soul. This is where I feel quiet peace.

This peace that lets me breathe without feeling the weight of the world on my chest. It quiets my mind and ceases the relentless questions I have about myself and where my artistic nature actually comes from. It quiets that ongoing question.

My mother's face today when the dr. said it's pancreatic cancer, so blank, the corners of her mouth upturned and poised.

She didn't move a muscle, staying in total intentional control.

This face I'm so familiar with.

Tonight, I'll paint her; I will paint her with a small little girl beside her.

The Mother is leaning on one knee bent down toward the child and the little child is looking up at her.

I place long brown strokes in the long locks of the mother's hair, and I move my brush to the little girl gently and carefully place small strokes of the same color for hints of similarities between them.

Next, I add small lashes to their big brown eyes where I smudge with my knuckle to blend and add dabs of white in the pupils of the little girl to show the light, the actual feeling she had for this woman, for her mother. The woman's lips are pressed on the forehead of the little girl for a kiss.

My mother's eyes are closed.

I paint her hands clasped together by her breast with her head tilted down for the kiss.

I create a shadow of pain in my mother's cheekbones giving her an expression that shows the beauty of the ache, the pain that only a mother can feel when loving a child and knowing that her child will never really know how deep her love is.

A love so great that it hurts a mother's heart, a pain as beautiful as anything she has ever experienced.

A pain called mothering.

I sit back in my chair and gaze at my progress.

I wonder if mother has ever known how to show this great love to anyone. I wonder why she never learned how or if she learned it then why didn't I feel it.

I wonder if, maybe, when she met my father, she was a different person. Did she show her heart? Was she ever vulnerable? Has she ever been spontaneous? Did she imagine more for herself?

I don't know the answers and maybe never will.

As for tonight, I need to rest because tomorrow will be a long day waiting with dad.

I will bring something for us to do to distract him, and I will be their rock because that is exactly what I was bred to be.

I am Samantha Jenkins, and the Jenkins women rise to every occasion.

I rinse my brushes out and set them on a dish towel beside the sink, then scoop up Leroy and walk to my bedroom and curl up with him in my blanket.

This feels so good.

The city lights and noise tonight are bright and lively, so much is happening on the street outside.

I shift my mind.

I have been practicing breathing techniques for years in order to fall asleep and it always works well. I learned it from a show I watched a long time ago and thought if these people can do it, I can as well.

I take one huge breath in, so very deep, almost filling up every inch of my lungs with air, then release it slowly and with every step of release, I relax and with steps in my mind focusing on my feet, then my legs, then my lower back into my shoulders, while letting my final air relax my facial muscles.

Usually, I am out for the night in one minute flat.

Tonight, I go through my routine and then as I am exhaling, I hear a loud siren screaming by my condo.

Immediately, and I don't know why, my mind goes back to the gallery and that rude man who was staring at my painting.

Why in the world am I thinking of him?

The man was so full of himself, but his cologne.

The smell of him made my heart go wild.

Chapter 7

Hospitals have never been my thing.

Most people say the scent alone is what keeps people away but for me, it's because I am simply so unfamiliar with them; I was always a healthy child, never needing to go to one. So being here makes me feel uneasy.

But, then again, look at hospital TV shows, always complete madness; Grey's Anatomy, The Resident, Scrubs, New Amsterdam.

They're ludicrous.

And because of this everyone thinks they have a medical degree because they watched fifteen seasons of Grey's Anatomy and can Google and DIY their healthcare.

This makes every 23 year old want to move to Seattle because they think McDreamy lives there. This new generation cracks me up. Sometimes I wonder if they know the difference between reality and pretend. I do think, however, these up and coming kids will keep me employed as an attorney. Perhaps, they are my job security.

My mind is moving in every direction thinking about hospitals. To add to the list of things that baffle the hell out of me is why do doctors wear white when there is so much bodily fluids involved in their daily work? Blood, vomit, and liquids that I can't even think about. But white uniforms? This never made much sense to me.

To my analytical mind, my life has nothing in common with hospitals and I like it that way. For now, it is about Mother.

Checking her into her room for pre-op is routine until a nurse walks us to a room with two beds, one with the curtain drawn, which can only mean mother has a roommate.

We three stare over at the empty bed where mom was asked to change and make herself comfortable, but nobody moves a muscle.

Suddenly, we hear a bout of coughing from the other side of the curtain, followed by a long moan.

Mom's roommate is very uncomfortable. She sounds miserable in pain.

I'm equal parts curious and alarmed by the sounds coming out of that patient.

I'm just about to ask the nurse if this woman needs help when mom catches her attention first. And very loud for the whole room to hear.

"Excuse me, dear? I prefer my own room, for privacy. If you would, be a wonderful employee and find me a single room." Not a question, not even a statement, but a clear demand.

I'm thinking, "Hi. This is my mom." But instead of talking I am going to let the nurse field this one, I'm not about to butt in.

I look over to see the ends of the nurse's mouth, uptick, just slightly.

I recognize that smirk.

I cock my head to the side a bit, take a seat at the end of the bed quietly, rest my chin in my hand, raise an eyebrow and become an audience member.

I've spent the last three years studying body language in the courtroom, and I can tell this nurse knows EXACTLY the kind of woman my mother is. I am certain she's up for a challenge.

"I apologize, Mrs. Jenkins, but I am unable to place you in a single. All beds are full and patients are forced to share rooms throughout the length of their care. Your care WILL BE impeccable and we will make sure you are as comfortable as you're accustomed to being throughout your stay." She gives mother a wink and pivots right out the door, not giving my mom a chance for a rebuttal, which is to me, a clear court room move.

My mother turns to me and gives a loud "tssssk".

At that, a giggle sounds from the other side of the curtain.

This stay is about to get interesting, I think to myself, You cannot make this up. Maybe next time I will bring popcorn.

Mom uses the shared bathroom and comes out in her hospital gown and we spend the next two hours with the team of nurses preparing her for her surgery.

Then mom sits in her blue Johnny on the bed in her housecoat and slippers.

I almost feel bad for her because I she almost appears vulnerable, with an IV in, waiting for her surgery.

She seems different to me, uneasy.

Maybe scared? I know Dad and I are.

My heart hurts and I feel for her; she's not in control and that might be the hardest thing about this, for her.

To fill in the awkward silence I feel the need to strike conversation up.

"Mother, is there anything I can get for you?" I ask and walk over to sit beside my mother, sure to be close enough for her but not too close for me.

Dad jumps in. "Yes, honey, can we get anything for you?" Backing up my plan to keep talking until she gets called in.

"Oh darling," she says, "of course not, I have all I need. I will be in and out of surgery before you know it and going home. I have arranged for Dottie to come over and make dinner for your father this evening and already prepared Roger to keep an eye on the house in case we're here longer. I have everything covered, aside from rescheduling the pool cleaning. I am certain I forgot to call them and it's due on Friday.Oh Dear"

She turns to me, "Samantha, you can have Dexter call and do this. Have him schedule me a hair appointment in two weeks. I am certain in two weeks my hair will need a touch-up," she says and touches the edges of her hair for good measure.

Are we kidding?! This is what's on her mind?

My mother is about to go into surgery for what could be an aggressive and serious form of cancer and by the way, I am pretty sure Dexter is NOT mother's assistant, nor is he in the business of making her hair appointments.

Heck, I am pretty sure he has never made one for me, although, he HAS suggested my taste in hair style leaves a lot to be desired.

Tucked over the ear and air-dried apparently does nothing for my looks if you ask Dexter.

But I don't say anything about that, I just say, "Yes mother."

I will take care of this myself, I would never ask Dexter to do this, but what she doesn't know won't kill her.

Hmmm.

Maybe a bad choice of words now.

"Very well, Samantha. Also, your birthday is coming up and I would like you to think of what you might like to do to celebrate. I was thinking of having a surprise 30th birthday party for you; we could invite all your friends and I will invite new ones. We'll have it catered and even have maybe a bit of entertainment poolside, perhaps even a live band. Then, you show up and act surprised. It would most certainly be a change of pace for you, something for you to *do*."

"Mother, *NO!*"

I realize I said that too quickly and immediately cover with, "Mother, you will still be recovering from surgery, and we need to get prepared for the treatment plan the doctors will have you on, starting in two weeks. We can eventually celebrate, but with my client load right now, I really can't commit to anything."

She loves this answer, and I know it; this is her ace in the hole, the same hand she plays with her girlfriends when they discuss their children.

"Oh, of course, Samantha. Yes, I agree. Your career is, and must remain, your focus. Speaking of focus; did you hear that Steven Edwards from high school, you know who I mean, he's in town and still single! He may be receiving an award for his work in technology. Evidently, he was nominated for an ORBIE award. His mother told me he'll be here for a week and would *love* to see some old friends. You're an *old* friend, don't you think, Samantha?"

She must remind me that he's single and I'm old.

"Sure, I'll reach out to him and see if he wants to have coffee. We follow each other on Instagram." I say with pain shooting straight up my nerves to my soar brain from thinking of this soon to be set-up date. I know how this starts. She has done this many times before.

Steven is a friend from school who was voted most likely to be on a ready-to-mingle-but-still-single type of dating site and he's not someone I'm interested in, but being a corporate attorney I'm pretty sure he could be a source of referrals. That's the upside? Maybe? No. I doubt it.

My train of thought is interrupted by a nurse coming into the room. "Okay, Eleanor, the operating room has called for you,"

I feel my stomach turn as the nurse comes in and lifts my mother's railing to lock her in for the ride.

'Oh, no." She says firmly. " I can walk. I am perfectly fine to walk to the room," Mother immediately pushes back.

"Mrs. Jenkins, we can't allow you to do that. It's hospital policy that all patients be wheeled in and prepped for surgery." She takes her foot, clicks the lever on the bed, causing mother to give a startled jump.

The nurse shoots her a sassy smile, and rolls Mother toward the door.

We hear another giggle from the other side of the curtain and mom's eyes roll. The other patient seems to be loving the show.

Dad scurries behind the bed as it turns the corner out of the room, "I love you, sweetheart! I will be here waiting for you."

He walks into the hallway outside the door, and watches as she's rolled into a doorway marked medical staff only.

He sighs big with a discouraging look and turns to me, then says, "Now what?"

I reach into my bag and yank out our cribbage board we've played on countless times before, "I brought this. Let's go to the waiting room and play. Winner buys lunch?"

Dad says, "Sure. Does that include ice cream?"

"You bet!" I say and wink at him.

It's my mission to keep Dad in a good space; cribbage always does this. He is the best and I know the best parts of me are from him.

We set up the pegs and decide I'm red and he's blue; we play at least six games as the hours roll on by.

The room fills up with people, then empties out; fills up, and empties again.

We pass the hours listening to conversations and we spend the better part of the morning playing and making eye contact over the conversations around us and grinning at each other.

My dad and I are always on the same page. Looking at him as I peg out and beat him for the 3rd time, I almost take a picture of him in my mind, hoping forever to never forget this very moment. This moment of being with him.

We check the clock every hour or two; it feels like days, but I knew it was only six hours since we last saw mom.

We didn't know the turn our lives were about to take.

Chapter 8

It feels like we've been waiting for days in that waiting room.

I've won 14 games while dad was sitting at about 8.

I have no cell service, so Dad and I just keep playing game after game and folks, also waiting in the waiting room, begin to come over and watch us play while some are sleeping, praying together and others are just staring at the clock.

A couple comes in holding hands and sits down. They sit down and she takes her head and rests it on his shoulder. I notice he leans over and kisses her forehead.

My mind wanders a bit as it has a million times before, watching couples in love.

Maybe they've been married ten years, maybe more, but they look young, probably in their thirties.

He is sweet to her.

His hand holds hers and I notice he lifts her hand and adjusts her wedding band, then looks at her and smiles.

They're cute.

Then I hear, "Walter Jenkins?"

The voice is coming from the entryway to the OR suites.

My eyes dart to the voice that startles me out of a game dad and I are in the middle of; something about that voice seems familiar.

The doctor says again, "Walter Jenkins".

I look at my father and quietly say, "Dad?"

My dad looks up and says "Oh yes over here. I'm sorry. Yes, over here. We're coming. My hearing isn't so good these days."

My dad scrambles putting everything in his bag and heads to the door where the doctor had summoned him.

As we walk over to the man, I'm almost hesitant, maybe even cautious.

Do I know him?

I look at him. hmmmm I think I know him.

But how? Who is he? Why does he look and sound so familiar? How in the world do I know this man?

"Follow me," he says and gestures to a corner of the room, where we sit with our full attention on him, both of us searching his eyes for what he might tell us.

"I'm Dr. Hayden Bryant," he says and shakes our hands.

"I'm assisting Dr. Piper on your wife's case. I believe he shared with you that I will be involved" he says, turning his body toward my father as he speaks to him.

"First, I want to say the surgery went well and Mrs. Jenkins is in recovery."

I can almost feel my dad's relief as his shoulders drop from right under his ears and finally relax.

"I apologize for the length of time you and your...". He looks over at me and dad starts to answer but I butt in.

"Samantha Jenkins, daughter. I'm their daughter."

He nods and hesitates, looks at me with his eyes squinting slightly as though trying to place me.

He seems to know me, too, but he carries on with his sentence with a nod of his head.

"Nice to meet you, Samantha. The surgery ended up being lengthy but only because we performed what we call the Whipple Procedure; Eleanor was a great candidate for this. She is healthy enough currently to recover from this well. In short, what we did was remove the head of the pancreas to prevent the tumors from moving to her other organs. It's the safest and best procedure for your wife and mother, " he looks to me and continues "We made a large incision in her abdomen area and removed the head of the pancreas where the tumors were located and connected what remained of the pancreas to the small intestine then reattached that to the stomach which allows for food to digest. "

He took a deep breath and continued.

"Pathology will determine if it's metastasized. While this is a significant surgery and known to have a very small chance of success, her recovery period is crucial and lengthy. Therefore, Eleanor will be with us here at the hospital for at least a week while we watch her for signs of infections and manage her pain, accordingly."

I am listening to him and feverishly scribbling notes in my notepad, my head spinning with all the medical jargon, although I'm sure I got all of it down.

"And now more about her recovery," he continues and as he does, I study him, trying to place him.

He's tan, about thirty-five, with a strong jawline and good teeth.

He's so familiar and I am suddenly convinced that it's not for a good reason.

Do I know him from the office?

Did I go against him in court?

This is absurd.

How in the world do I know him?

Focus Samantha, I think and force myself to listen to his instructions.

"She'll be on a liquid diet until we can re-introduce solids in a couple of days, depending on her recovery. She will be heavily sedated to manage her pain and keep her as comfortable as possible. Our patient care here is top-notch, but I have found patients recover even better when a loved one is with them. One of you should consider being here during the day with her while she recovers."

This catches my attention.

"Wait, excuse me," I interject, "The entire day? Every day that she's here?"

"If possible, yes," his eyes shift to me, and I almost sense a snarky reply and a grin behind his lips.

I wait a moment, thinking he's going to continue but he stays quiet, waiting for me to continue.

I mean. . . is that a question he was asking? A statement? Does he personally want to know if I'm going to be here?

There's something about this guy that makes my head spin, something about the way he looks, I'm not sure why.

Pull it together, Samantha, I scream in my head.

"Um, well, my father," I clear my throat, "my father, here, this is my father. He is a professor, and his schedule is tight. So. Well. I can be here," I clear my throat, "I mean I can try. But I'm not sure if I can do it all day. "

I'm struggling to speak concisely.

"I am certain I can be here every day, or try to, anyway. I mean, I can work from here. I am an attorney so my caseload *can* be sent to me."

I'm stumbling.

Why can't I speak?

Something about this guy rocks me in a very bad way And I can tell he's enjoying it because there is no way for him to wipe that smug smirk from his lips.

My asshole radar starts going off.

Pull it together, Samantha and *fast, this guy is on to me*!

"OK. I can be here," I spit out.

"Wonderful!" He says, "Good to know," as he nods his head up and down with exaggeration.

Finally, I'm getting back on track.

"We will be seeing a lot of you, then… Samantha?"

Shit. Is that another question or a statement?

"Yes, you will," I answer too quickly with a confidence I don't feel.

And with that, Dr. Hayden Bryant grabs his clipboard, shakes dad's hand, and turns in his white coat and fancy shoes to leave.

Just then a breeze from the door closing behind him sends a waft of his scent my way. It hits me like a frigid day in winter.

That smell, his cologne; now, that's familiar.

My dad looks over at me and says, "Oh Sammy, your mother is going to be so upset she can't recover at home. I hope they tell her, and we don't have to! I will need to call the school and tell them she needs me, Sam. I must ask for some time off, maybe even the entire semester."

Dad is panicking and I need to reassure him I'm here.

"Dad," I rest my hand on his, squeeze and say softly, "we got this. I can be with mother while you work. I have Dexter at the office sending me work and I will be here with her at the same time. I will absolutely call you if I need you, in a heartbeat. Dad, I have this."

I feel him relax.

My dad is the best, gentlest, man I've ever known with the biggest heart.

My mother was blessed to have found him.

He is patient and kind.

He, no matter what, has always made sure we knew how much he loves his girls.

I cannot imagine our lives without this man.

Growing up with such opposite parents, at times, was confusing but for me, I always know how much he loved us.

He always makes sure we know.

It's time for me to pay this man back; I must step up and be there for him, for them.

And honestly, if thinking of me sitting with my mom while I work and she recovers gives him a sense of comfort, I owe it to him.

It will also keep me informed about her health.

But mom is a strong woman, and I can bet she'll be better sooner than Dr. Fancy Shoes Bryant says she will.

I have a better sense of her strength and know we will blow this Doc out of the water and be ready to go home sooner than he thinks!

It could very well be dad I will need to take care of most; she is his love and without her, he would be lost.

I turn to dad to give him reassurance, "Dad, Mom is going to beast mode herself through this. You and I will be here and work through it with her. She's strong." I give him a nudge and a smile.

"Dad, come on! Remember when I was eight years old when mom and I went to the choral recital at my school?"

Dad starts laughing, he already knows where I'm going with this.

"And I was on stage singing that Annie song and I stopped right in the middle because I got scared? I froze, and there was dead silence in the audience. You could have heard a pin drop! And then a bunch of kids started laughing at me? And yup before we knew it, mom stood up and started giving the kids hell, RIGHT IN THE MIDDLE of the auditorium! I could have crawled under a chair!"

I start to imitate her with my finger waving in the air, "Stop that right now. Shame on you laughing at my daughter when you aren't even on stage or dare to, yourselves. Shame on you! And she gave them the longest death scare with her eyes popping right out. Remember that, Dad?"

I look at my dad and bug my eyes out just like she did that day, exaggerated and latently insane.

We're dying as we remember, tears welling up and running down our faces as we laugh hysterically.

My dad is waving his finger like I did.

Mom had courage and bravery and she also never hesitated to call anyone on anything.

'Dad, those boys zipped their lips right up and looked down at the floor, I couldn't believe it! I'm telling you. Those boys never looked me in the eye when we went back to school, her death stare was in their minds forever. And she wonders why I never really dated in high school."

"Samantha, I think I even looked down along with those shits!" Dad adds and we both belt out our laughter.

Mom just has that way about her.

Whenever we aren't sure what she's feeling (or if she even has feelings), she takes a hard right and mama bear comes raring out, claws bared and at the ready.

At this moment, I feel guilty.

Guilty for having no patience when she took my ChapStick out of my purse and put lipstick in its place.

Guilty for every time she took my napkin at dinner time and placed it on my lap as though I had forgotten my manners as an adult.

Guilty for wishing she wasn't my mother growing up whenever I saw my friends' moms cuddle with them.

She really does love me, but maybe her way of showing it isn't a way that I see as loving.

Suddenly I feel the need to let my dad know something.

I look at him and take his hand in mine, hold it like he has always held mine when I need him, and level my gaze with his.

"Dad, I love you, I know I often forget to visit and forget to call because of how busy life is. I love you and Mother, and I need you to know how much you both mean to me."

I see dad's eyes fill and a tear rolls down his cheek.

"Sammy; we know this. We love you so much, too. I also love how you are the most beautiful part of your mother and the best of me. Sweetheart, every day, your mother and I discuss how proud we are of you. And not once do we think you are too busy for us. We know you're building your life and we love watching you grow into the woman you are."

"Daddy, I love you," I wrap my arms around the neck of this great man that I get to call my father, a man that gave me the standard of what a real man is.

He has never left our side, he is devoted to this family, dedicated to his job and never once have I heard him complain or speak ill of anyone.

What man could fill his shoes?

This man is my daddy, and I love him.

Meanwhile, as I'm hugging dad, my eyes shoot to the waiting room door.

Who is this Dr. Bryant and why am I so drawn to him?

And why does he ride my nerves at the same time?

Chapter 9

I knock as gently as I can on the door of her room in case she's resting; it's only been one day since her surgery, and I know she's tired.

"Come in," a voice says, raspy from years of smoking, that certainly isn't my mom.

I slowly walk in and say quietly, "Hello?"

I walk into the room and in front of me in the bed is not my mother but an older woman maybe in her 70's or 80's, thin and frail, but with a raspy voice that's almost manly.

She holds a pen in her left hand, poised as though it's a cigarette dangling from her fingers.

She looks me over and says, "*You* must belong to *her*," and gestures toward the other side of the room with a jerk of her thumb.

"Um, yes? Is she still in this room?" I ask, intimidated by her attitude and that voice.

"Yeah, the lady is out cold. She was up all night complaining about being too close to the door, couldn't shut her up until I finally said the hell with it and switched places with her. Now she's sleeping like a baby."

I walk past her giving her a careful smile and a nod of thanks. This woman scares me slightly.

But She is correct.

Mom is sleeping peacefully with a blood pressure cuff on one arm and an IV line in the other; there are oxygen tubes in her nose.

None of this can be comfortable, even with the meds.

I find a seat at the foot of her bed and make a mental note to grab a quilt from home for her legs.

Day one of seven, I think to myself.

Hopefully this week flies by.

I hear buzzing from my jacket pocket and the old lady across the room mumbles under her breath that I'm just like my mother.

I grab my phone; it's Dexter.

"Hey Dex," I answered, trying hard to be quiet.

"Morning, morning! I'm at the office and you are never going to believe what Gary did!" Dexter is bright eyed, and bushy tailed, ready to jump right into discussing work gossip.

Gary is another paralegal in the office and once he started working for the firm, Dexter was immediately ready for the competition for firm drama queen.

I smile at the normalcy; we like this.

"Tell me," I ask, entertaining him.

Dexter jumps right in, "Well, you know how for months that damn Pay Snack Box in the employee break room has been short on money. And I *told you* I thought it was Gary. Well…. bingo! I caught him red-handed. He was reaching for a Snickers bar and surer than shit, he didn't drop even one dime into the pay box."

Oh boy; Dexter's on a roll. It doesn't help that he's right.

"Dex, really? An employee snack box? Gary? What if he was going to pay it back later? I mean I've done that tons of times myself."

I must defend poor Gary; he tries so hard to fit in.

He's maybe 5'2" and is a cross between Danny DeVito and George Costanza, with a personality that matches both.

Poor Gary; he struggles.

"Sam, are you for real? He IS the thief of our Snack Box. GURL! I caught him red-handed."

I'm dying, he's so funny, and I'm going to let him enjoy this moment.

It's also exactly what I needed.

I say my goodbyes and offer good luck after he gives me notes on client files, I hang up and smile.

I love him, he's a good guy.

Right in the middle of me cheese-smiling, Dr. Bryant walks in and pulls the curtain back with a chipper, "Good morning ladies!"

He notices mother sleeping and lowers his voice then repeats, "Good morning," to only me.

"Morning, Doctor. Um, Dr. Bryant." I wrestle with my phone and turn it off, fumbling through it, then stand up.

"Ms. Jenkins," his voice now almost whispers and asks me, "can we talk in the hallway?"

My heart free falls, "Yes. Yes, sure, ok," I say and follow him out.

We head toward the nurse's station, and he sets his clipboard down on the counter, then turns his whole body to me and says, "We received your mothers pathology report this morning."

I feel my heart pounding through my chest because he's scaring me.

He reads my face and reaches his hand over to my arm and gently says, "Ms. Jenkins, let's find a place to sit."

His voice is calm and I need that at this moment because I am not so sure what he is about to tell me.

"Please, call me Samantha," but he dismisses what I say.

"I know it's been a whirlwind for your family; your mother's surgery *did* go very well, the best it could. But we need to remember the next three days are crucial while her body undergoes a great deal of healing. As you know, your mother had tumors eligible for resection, which is the best kind on the pancreatic cancer scale, if there is such a scenario. Going into the surgery yesterday, our biggest challenge was the cancer finding its way into her veins, which is *not* the case, so we're relieved. This classifies the tumors as T2 measuring slightly over 2cm. Keep in mind, we did extract her lymph nodes during surgery, which is a common procedure to eliminate cancer spreading to them. We extracted 22 Lymph nodes and sent them to pathology, and we received the results this morning and discovered 6 out of 22 Lymph nodes tested came back cancerous. This places your mom's cancer at Stage 3."

This sounds to me like supercalifragilisticexpialidocious, complete gibberish.

This doctor knows nothing about getting to the point; has he never heard the expression "in a nutshell"?

He's being careful not to get to the point.

It all seems so difficult to not only understand but to process because all I heard was the word cancer.

None of this makes sense to me.

"No. Dr. Bryant, I don't understand, she was so healthy. I…" I'm shaking my head in disbelief.

Why? She was healthy, she was normal…well as normal as she could be and now, I think to myself.

"Ms. Jenkins, I know this is difficult. It won't get any easier throughout the process from healing to treatment, and beyond. And I don't know your mom very well, but she seems like a tough cookie."

This makes me smirk.

A tough cookie.

I suppose that is a perfect way to describe her; he's being kind, calling her that and not something else altogether, which he could.

"It may have appeared that your mom was fine, but I am confident your mom was in pain for quite some time and didn't alert anyone. There is absolutely no way she felt no pain. I see this far too much in your parents' generation. We need to understand that our parents and grandparents didn't grow up the way we have. They grew up going to doctors *far less* than we did and resorted to being outdoors and getting fresh air to cure any type of illnesses and ailments. Being sick for our parents' generation is more of an insult and an embarrassment than it is a life sentence or something to seek treatment and help for."

I feel the blood drop to my feet; I know this is hard but I'm trying to wrap my brain around this whole thing.

He continues, "I'm having this conversation with you to prepare you, so you and I can be there for your parents as they navigate the next couple of days. I spoke with your folks earlier, and thought it was important to speak directly to you."

He's careful how he speaks to me, very professionally, yet there's something about his eyes that tell me he's trusting me to do my part and be there for him.

He has a slight accent, almost like a Boston accent but not as thick; he barely pronounces his R's and it's kind of charming.

"You spoke to them, already? Were they ok? How did they react?" I ask, my tone rushed.

"Your dad took the news very well and your mom was very nonchalant about the results. Your father took down notes so I suspect he will be researching all of this today; I encourage you to keep an eye on him. The internet can be brutal and oftentimes diagnoses like this sound very tragic when they could very well be manageable. That's one of the reasons I speak directly to the family, to keep an eye on the patient's spouse because it can feel very daunting for them both."

"Ok, Dr. Bryant. Thank you and I appreciate all you've done," I thank him, stand, and shake his hand.

He stands too, clasps my hand, and smiles, "You're welcome. I'm here all day today and on-call tomorrow morning if you need anything. The nurse's station can page me."

I walk back into mother's room and right before I step into the room I hear her speaking to someone.

She's awake. Her voice is weak, but I catch some of what she's saying.

"Oh, yes, I do know. But I have only five days and then I can go there myself and pick it up," she says.

I walk in and my mother looks up at me startled, then tucks her cell phone right into her side as though she was surprised by me being there.

"Hello mother! Everything ok?" I stand right beside her hospital bed and peer down at her.

Mom clears her throat, "Samantha," she says in greeting, then, "Just a business call I had to tend to."

Mother says in a stern but weak voice, "Where have *you* been? I've been calling the nurse's station for well over half an hour and they should have been here by now, so should you. I need to know if there are any flowers that have come in my name."

She moves aside slightly and moans but smiles as best she can and pats a little spot next to her on the bed, almost like an invitation to sit near her.

So, I accept and sit on her bed.

"Well, Mother, if there are flowers then they will bring them to you." I tell her, almost like I am talking with a child explaining why she wasn't given an invitation.

"Well, hmm, I guess next time anyone in my group is hospitalized I shall think twice before I send flowers to *them*," And there you have it; my mother. Sounds to me like she is getting a tad better.

But she *did* invite me to sit beside her, so I tentatively take the space she made for me.

It's a gesture that's uncomfortable for me to witness, her patting the bed for me to come and sit. She has never been an affectionate woman and, to be honest, not many get too close knowing she was not the hugging type, ever.

·I sit down and find it to be slightly uncomfortable, but it warms me, a feeling I, too, am not quite sure of.

I look at her.

She's pale, hooked up to all kinds of machines that make her look, for the first time in her life, vulnerable.

This woman is having to rely on someone other than herself and I can imagine it can be difficult for her… and for them.

This woman, my mother, is at war with needing help and accepting help.

I look down at her hands.

I never noticed before how old she's getting.

The skin on the tops of her hands looks thin and even thinner with the pulse/ox monitor on her finger.

My eyes follow her long fingers; I never noticed before, but my hands resemble hers to an eerie degree.

She has long elegant hands suited for piano playing, with long nail beds.

I've never liked my hands.

Everyone says I should be playing an instrument with hands like mine or playing basketball but in this moment, in this very moment realizing I have something of hers, I like them.

Her hands.

In that moment, she places her hand on mine; I can't say I didn't jump but I can say it makes me look up at her in disbelief.

Her hands feel cold.

"Mom, I..." She notices my surprised face and grabs my fingers in hers, brings them to her eyes and looks at my nails.

"Samantha, look at those nails! You need to stop chewing your cuticles. They look a mess. I have lotion in my purse, grab some and get those nail beds moisturized," and she pulls her body back at what looks like stomach pain, and she grimaces.

She is in pain, doing too much and saying too much, and she still motions me to her purse in the corner.

And I think, for a minute, she's going to tell me she loves me or thank me for being here but instead she sees a flaw... forget it.

My mind can't go there.

I get up and grab her purse and rummage through it.

I feel around and immediately find something in the side pocket I haven't seen in a long time, a little ring I wore as a child.

It's on her key ring with her house key and another that I don't recognize.

Interesting.

Why, I wonder?

All these years, she kept the ring dad gave me when I started school; I thought that ring was long gone after I outgrew it.

I find her lotion and pull it out; I look at my mother as she watches me with her glasses resting on the end of her nose.

And for a moment, without thinking, I stand up, walk back to mother's bedside, sit down, squirt the lotion into my palm and moisturize my fingers, then grab hers and rub the extra from my own hands into her skin.

I look up at her and it's almost like she's holding her breath watching me in disbelief as I rub the lotion into her hands.

"Mother," I say, "You're in Pain and you need to rest. We're worried you aren't taking this seriously. Also, Mother, I spoke to your doctor, and he said he talked to you. So, I want to let you know that while you will be here a little bit longer, so will I. It's important you stay here for about a week for rest and monitoring, but you do have to rest. The risk of infection is too high if you don't. It's also important that if they offer you pain medicine, you take it."

I'm clear with her because she needs to understand the gravity of all of this.

But of course, mother is mother, and she answers with, "Don't you worry one bit about me. Samantha," and pulls her hands away.

"I will be home before your father knows it and I'm not someone who needs painkillers," she snaps out, her voice rising so her neighbor can hear and says, "Not like someone else in this room."

"MOTHER!" I mouth, appalled.

And then, just as I'm praying her roommate is sleeping, we hear from the other side of the curtain, her neighbor's raspy voice snapback, "I need my pain killers more than ever. since you arrived, *Queen Elizabeth.*"

Chapter 10

I must say that I have more sympathy now than I ever have for employees that were called into work because of a sick relative in the past.

I never could relate to the unpredictable time off with employees at the office; appointments, their kids sick at school, their relatives that passed or the subsequent funeral arrangements.

I'd never encountered tragedy or anything that had our family frantically making any type of personal arrangements or having to take time off work.

We go to work, we show up no matter what, it's how I was raised.

It was an expectation; almost a culture.

Truly, our lives just kind of happened around that mindframe.

We put everything we have into school, jobs, events and as a family, we're all-in if it has anything to do with working and the one leading the pack was of course, my mother.

She always has things in place, so we've never *had* to worry about the bigger picture things that could prevent us from working.

She did this so that we could create big things of our own. I suppose she always wanted me to succeed and so I never stopped trying.

As controlling as that sounds, it allowed dad to work hard at the university and that was our way of living.

I can say this; *he* included me in his work. I was on standby at the university waiting for classes to finish so he and I could spend time together on our way home, stopping at fun places that any 10-year-old would think are the coolest.

Mother did her part and always made sure we had what we needed, when needed, and lined up all contacts necessary for our successes.

And, so, while she may not have hugged me, and spent an inordinate amount of time correcting me, I know she loves me through her ways.

She opened doors to tremendous opportunities for me.

The best private schools that others couldn't get into, the best job shadowing at firms I never thought possible; she connected me to the people I needed to meet in order to get into the best college and thrive.

She arranged everything in my life.

Mother has always gotten things done and I never questioned a thing.

She just magically knew what she wanted for us, for me, and kept clear of any obstacles that would interrupt me from working hard.

It worked, or so I thought.

I do find, now as an adult, I get into my own head and wonder where I would be, what I would be, if I had grown up like the students I saw at Dad's school.

I admit, sometimes I get lost in that fantasy of normalcy.

I appreciate and love my mom; she is a mother through and through.

That umbilical cord doesn't have stretch reach between us. Yes, she is annoying as all hell with her directness, her instinct to speak right from the top of her head without filtering, and she always made sure I knew what I needed to do to be better by telling me my shortcomings.

No doubt she was strict, but never mean, never in a way that made me angry at her.

As a teen it elicited a roll of the eyes kind of response; as an adult, growing up in our family, it has made me content living and being alone and not diving into having a family of my own.

But with all those things that I complain about, I knew this for sure, she loves me. She loves to help others, as well.

She gave everything she has to every charity that she inherited from her father, and she volunteered endless hours at the local homeless shelter. She grew up with money and when Papa and Mimi passed, as a single child, she received enough to never need to work after I was born.

Instead, she and dad moved back to the city where she kept all her father's business contacts and took the lead on most of the larger benefits and charities in the area.

She's good at what she does.

She organized it all and mostly on the dime of her trust; raising money for other charities became her full-time occupation. She was not necessarily great at hugging or expressing love, being capable of being close, but she *is* a good woman.

Shoes I suspect I can, and will, never fill.

Growing up I could see by the looks on the faces of her friends that they thought she was hard on me because it wasn't their norm or how they would do it.

She's always quick to notice things that need fixing like my hair, my clothes, the car I drive, and especially the few men I took home to meet them.

But she does have a heart. One just has to tilt their head sideways to see it. But it's there.

We see this when we catch glimpses of how she shares herself with others and for others. Growing up I would watch her slip hundred-dollar bills into an envelope that she would seal and ask me to give it to the owner of the diner where dad and I went together after classes. Mr. Jalbert had owned the diner since mother and dad were young and dating and dad said it was their date spot.

Mr. Jalbert was a frail older man whose wife died years ago, and the diner was run down but always a stop for dad and me. We saw the same faces whenever we ate there.

So, when I was in high school and walking to school with my friends, she asked me to drop the envelopes like that off, regularly.

It was only when I was a senior in high school that it became obvious that my mother was giving Mr. Jalbert money to help him. I never really knew why I was making the drop-off for her, just that when he saw me, his face lit up and without skipping a beat he would say when handed it to him, "Bless you."

Mother has heart, she just keeps it behind a curtain for no one to see.

As I'm sitting here staring at her lying in bed, looking weak and frail and not getting stronger as expected, I'm starting to think of her mother having her as a young child, as a teen, heck as a woman my age.

What had hardened my mother to the point where her goodness was so private, where it became rare to share her heart openly?

What made her so passionate about *my* successes and what I must learn to do right?

How did she get to the point in her life where she needed everything to be perfect?

And *why*?

I may not ever know these answers, but for now I'm sitting here trying to make sense of how-to best care for her rather than the other way around.

How in the world did I miss the fact that she was getting old when I am so conscious that I'm aging too?

My mind is spinning in circles, it's all so confusing, but what I do know is this; I might never really know my mom's heart.

I also may not know who I am and where I came from because she has always been so hard to understand.

As a college student, I had discussions with friends who shared that they found themselves because they knew the kind of woman THEY came from. They knew their mother and because of that, they knew themselves better.

This will never be the case for me, it's something I will never have.

This was foreign to me, a different language.

This is likely why I find myself floundering in dating, roaming around at the gallery slinging my paintings secretly while trying my best at the firm.

Three very different directions. Three different lifestyles. Three different worlds I live in.

I can't find myself because I don't know at all who this woman, my mother, is.

Or maybe I am *way* overthinking.

I exhale and stand up; I need to get out of my head.

It's late and I need to go home; I've thought myself into a dark hole and home in bed is the best place for me tonight.

The nurse comes in and asks me if it's ok to dim the lights and if I need anything else.

"You look tired, Ms. Jenkins, you should really get home and rest; you and your father have been here for four straight days with your mom, rotating schedules. We'll call you if we need you for anything," she reassures me, and I know she is right and she will.

"Thank you so much, yes, please call me if you need anything. I keep my phone on all night," I say as I pack up my sketch pad and pencils, "I'll be back in the morning. I must stop by the office but *will* be here by 9am."

"Of course. We'll call if anything changes; go get some rest."

"Thank you, I will." I walk over to mom; her breathing is nice and calm, her mouth open.

She is finally getting rest.

She used to tell me when I was little that when we rest, we heal, and that's why we should never make decisions right away, that we should always sleep on it.

Mom and her little tips on life; I smile and lightly kiss her forehead, then whisper, "Bye mother, I love you."

I pass her roommate, who's watching Wheel of Fortune on her TV.

She looks at me and with her two fingers, she gives me a silent salute.

I smile at her because makes me laugh and leave.

I walk past the nurse's station where the younger nurse who's been helping mother is.

"Bye!" She says, chipper with her Southern accent, despite it being 8pm and she's been here since I got here at here early this morning.

"Bye, ladies, have a good night," I tell them and push the elevator to go down to the parking garage.

On my way down in the elevator, I lean against the elevator wall.

I. Am. Exh*austed*.

Mentally and physically.

I'm ready for bed.

I close my eyes thinking about the sketch I started while sitting at Mom's bedside. I always wanted to sketch a husband and wife that were well into their elder years; I wanted to sketch them sitting on children's swings beside one another, holding hands, their hair peppered with silver, their hands clinging together and their legs pumping together as they moved in sync on their swings.

In my mind their story is that they met when they were kids and always found themselves back at the swings and playground where they grew up together.

Their story.

I always find beauty in watching couples but elderly couples with their wrinkled hands and lines that defined every day they worked hard, every child they held, and every heart they touched inspired me the most.

Elderly people always have stories, good stories that they turned into lessons and drawing their skin, their hands, their expressions, always creates a story to share.

In the last couple of days in Mom's hospital room, and outside in the common area, I started this drawing. It pulled me into another world, momentarily, and it felt like an escape, maybe even a romantic one. It gave me a job, something to do because sitting idle has never been my strong suit, I need to keep busy, and my brain needs this movement.

I feel the elevator hit the ground level with a thud, and the door opens while I'm still in deep thought.

I lean down and grab my bag, start to walk out of the elevator and into the parking garage and as I turn the corner my body slams into someone. I feel the wind get knocked out of me and in slow motion I bend over, catching my breath.

"What the hell?" I say, fully ready to interrogate somebody a new one.

"Oh, gosh, I'm so sorry!" A man is picking up my bag that was knocked open, mom's medical papers flying and my pencils scattering everywhere.

This guy collects the papers as fast as he can, and then looks up at me.

"Ms. Jenkins? Oh, my word, I'm sorry, I didn't see you coming. I was on my way back to the floor because I forgot something. I'm so, so…wait…. are you ok?"

He reads my face and I'm pretty sure I have a face that's shock mixed with slight pain; I can see the stars swirling around from when we hit, we collided hard.

 "Are you ok? Come here, sit down," He brings me to a bench near the elevator and guides me to sit.

I kind of shake my head slowly, like I'm trying to get my bearings. I start to breathe easier, but this guy is a solid wall.

And well…. I hit him hard. What the hell is he made of …steel?

But steel doesn't usually smell this good.

I look at him and it registers.

"Oh shit; Dr. Bryant?" I squint my eyes at him because what the hell? This is Mom's doctor. Can my shitty day get any worse?

"I am so very sorry, "he repeats.

"No, no I'M sorry. I wasn't paying attention, I just walked out with my head in the clouds and… anyway, it's been a long day," I mumble trying to collect myself.

"Are you sure you're ok?" he asks.

I try to get up from the bench and stumble back to a seat, and smile weakly, "Yeah, I thought I was." I shake my head to clear it, "Oh and can you call me Samantha? Ms. Jenkins feels like something a teacher would call me."

He smirks, picking up on my humor.

I pull myself together feeling *very* foolish. I reach for my bag and remember the juice from earlier waiting in my bag. I pull out my OJ and take a quick drink, thinking I need to get out of this place.

I'm making a fool of myself.

'Here, Samantha," he says, emphasizing my name, as he helps me stand, "let's get you up and walk a little."

He places a finger on my wrist, checking my pulse; I look down and reassure him because this feels ridiculous.

"Honestly, I'm fine, Dr. Bryant." I catch a whiff of his scent and feel my pulse pick up; he smells more than good.

"Well, you appear to be as stubborn as your mother, but *you* can call me Hayden," he says.

"Watch out, my mother raised me, and stubborn is an understatement," I tilt my head and smirk back.

My middle name is Sassy and he's about to find that out.

He looks like he's trying to resolve an inner conflict and lowers his voice, "Look, I haven't eaten all day and I am starving. Something tells me you are too after eating cafeteria food all day, why don't you join me for a bite to eat over at Sully's? It's only a block away."

I look at him and say nothing because I'm not sure what he's asking.

So, I say, with hesitancy "Is that ok? My mother is your patient, I mean, is that weird?"

I'm pretty sure doctors have a code, right? Same as attorneys, only stricter?

I think to myself, *Buddy, is this your way of hitting on me because you need to improve your way of picking up women.*

He answers, "I'm safe," And slowly says with slight sarcasm, "It's just dinner," and holds both hands up like I have him at gunpoint. "I promise I'm not a serial doctor kidnapping my patients' daughters and I am pretty sure we are past that, anyway. You hit me like a wall!" He says and laughs.

"Touché," I throw back and smirk.

What the hell do I do other than just go?

I'm an adult, we both are.

And he is making it crystal clear that this is not a date.

Part of me is saying no, this is not appropriate to go out with your mother's doctor, and the other part of me is telling myself not to flatter myself, we're not suited for each other.

He could as easily be nice as he could be a weirdo.

Oh, the hell with it, I'm a grown woman, so I say, "Yeah, I guess. *Wait*. You know what? Yes. Yes, let's go. I *am* starving. I could eat a horse! Well not a full-grown horse, maybe a calf. Wait, that's not a baby horse, that's a baby cow."

Shit, here I go again with that nervous ramble.

What the hell is up with this guy? And why am I turning into an idiot suddenly?

He cuts me off knowing it's necessary, "Let's go, Samantha," saying my name like he's proud to call me by my name.

This guy is weird and if this is flirting, he sucks at it.

Wait, flirting? What am I thinking? He's just being nice. *Why* do I always assume guys are only wanting to flirt? Samantha, get a hold of yourself.

We walk out of the parking garage toward Sully's Grille and into the chilly NYC evening.

I can immediately tell that he is a gentleman. I'm still unsteady, and he has his arm hovering behind me but not touching the lower part of my back while we walk.

"So, tell me about your job. Did you have surgery today? I mean not you but your patients? Do you do many surgeries in a day?" I ask, trying to fill any potential awkward silences. I have no idea how to talk like a doctor but am trying my best.

"Yes. I usually have no more than two surgeries daily and Dr. Piper and I rotate schedules. He's pretty close to retiring so I am basically learning his daily caseload while he creates an exit plan," he says.

Impressive.

"Wow. That's a great opportunity for you, how long have you been practicing?" I ask; if I can piece together a timeline then I can figure out how old Hayden is.

"You want to know my age, don't you?" he asks bluntly.

"What makes you think that?" I ask and laugh nervously because, shit this guy is on to me.

"I'm 32," he says proudly.

"Well, congrats!" And we both laugh. "But you're much older than me! I'm 29," I tell him.

"Wow, you are just a baby" he banters back, and we laugh until it goes quiet.

"Some days it feels like I am about 22 while other days I am in bed by eight pm like an old lady. I don't know. Maybe a part of me is an old soul while another part of me is ready to get out there and live life to the fullest."

Why am I oversharing!? I shoot a look at him and hope he doesn't think I'm weird.

I never do this, ever, and I'm rusty.

But he catches what I am saying and calmly says, "Yeah, I get it. I can feel surgery is getting hard on my body but then I grab my dog and go backpacking up Mount Washington. I'm not sure what 32 looks like anymore. I'm tired, I'm awake. I'm hiking, I'm exhausted. It's a roller coaster. Take your mom, for example. I would never have guessed she's in her late 60's, she looks great, acts young. She is as spicy as the day is long. I would have given her early 50's, easily."

I'm laughing, "Oh, she would love to hear *that*! Mount Washington? Ok, look, I suck at geography but that's in New England, right?"

We reach the pub with its flashing sign with light bulbs that need replacing but still reads Sully's Bar and Grille. I look up at the sign for a long moment and Hayden laughs, "Don't worry. It's safe."

We've no sooner stepped inside than the bartender calls out, "Hayden! Glass of Pinot Noir?"

Hayden leads me toward a booth he says, "Yeah, Frankie, that'll be great; can I get a steak and cheese sub, too?"

He looks at me, a question in his eyes and I say, "A Sloe Gin Fizz and Frankie, make that two steak and cheese subs, please."

Hayden busts out laughing and slides into a booth to sit, "You and Frankie old friends?" I ask.

He winks at me and says, "Yeah, we drink like old people. Sloe gin fizz? I haven't seen a drink like that ordered since my grandmother had one at our family reunion."

"I get that a lot. My friend, Dexter, tells me in my last life I was a crotchety old lady that stayed home alone knitting and complaining about the neighbors and their barking dog. And I tell him, he *is* the neighbor I complain about." I say as I slide into the seat right across from Hayden in this leather booth with seats full of duct tape.

"Well, it sounds like your friend is a practical kind of guy. *But,* I have a sneaking suspicion I was the old man who lived upstairs from you with his dog."

He's charming, and comfortable enough to suggest we were neighbors in our last life.

This is weird, but. . . I like our banter.

He's easy to talk to; I bet he's gay.

Well, here's the good news, if he is, Dexter would love him, and I can play matchmaker.

Frankie drops our drinks on the table and immediately I take a hefty sip, "Hey, slow down. You just got the wind knocked out of you. Let's eat first" he says, his voice teasing.

"Oh, I see where this is going. Avoiding a lawsuit are you? Let me play whack a mole by body slamming my patient's daughter and then buy her dinner. This right here would *never* stand up in court," I tease back.

"You're on to me! Yowzah." he says.

What? "Wait, what did you just say? "I ask him, not believing my ears.

"You're on to me?" He asks.

"No, the other thing," I tilt my head and ask, laughter bubbling up in my throat, threatening to spill out.

"Yowzah?" He asks when he repeats it.

"Yup. Good Gosh You're *old*! Who says Yowzah under 50!? What else do you say? Jiminy Crickets?" I burst out laughing.

He laughs and shakes his head and asks, "Are you always like this?"

I shrug my shoulders and smirk.

We talk for a while, starting with where he's from.

"New Hampshire. I grew up in Massachusetts in foster care but at nine was placed with a family in New Hampshire who struggled with having children. They ended up having two children of their own with fertility specialists and decided against continuing biologically and to go through foster care, which is how they found me. So, I ended up being adopted at 12 years old. The court approved the adoption, and they became my family."

I take a deep breath. That's a lot and he kind of laid that out quickly. *But why*, I wonder. *Why does he want to share this with me?*

"Oh! You were a foster child?" I think for a minute. He's an over-sharer, too. I would have never pegged this guy as someone grew up in the system. He's so open and the attorney in me wants to know more.

"So, do you know your biological parents? If you don't mind me asking."

"Yes, I do. I was with them until I was five, but they were in a car accident one night and my father didn't make it. My mother ended up paralyzed, so she was unable to raise me. She is paraplegic and lives in a group home; she doesn't know one day from the other, so she never really came back from the accident," he says quietly.

"Oh, Hayden I am so sorry. I didn't mean to bring this up such a sensitive subject." Clearly I shouldn't have asked, and I feel like an ass.

'No, don't." He puts his hand up, "My parents are *amazing* and brought me to visit her often. We've always been open about my birth mother and my mom always made sure to keep my biological parents' memory alive with pictures. Look, they are awesome. You know what she did when I was little? She made me an album to document the life I had before the accident, and it became our bedtime story; it really helped me sleep in the beginning. Yeah, they were good to me. I think I'm very lucky, some would say blessed. I am open to talking about it and at any chance, I will, happily. I go to the rec center downtown to see the kids there and talk to them about life because a lot of them have had hard lives away from their parents and I try to help as much as I can. I share my knowledge about life and that I was placed with good people, because I held on. Those kids down there have nothing; they need hope. If I can give them half of what my parents gave me then I will pay it forward, right?"

"Hayden. . ." I say his name in awe; this guy is a saint, "Giving back is beyond good, it's everything that matters."

I'm blabbering again, I'm sure he can tell I'm nervous.

He reaches over and places his hand on my arm and says with a soft smile, "It's ok. I like to talk about it. I'm very open about my life. Some people have had hard lives and can change others while some people live high on the hog with a silver spoon in their mouths and never learn to appreciate how special life is. So don't worry; I like to talk about this."

At this moment I feel terrible because he kind of just described me.

High on the hog. Maybe not that exactly, but I haven't ever had to worry about things, so I boldly ask, "Because I live with a silver spoon?"

I don't mean to sound combative at all; I ask because It's true.

"Oh no! No, that's not what I meant, at all! Please don't think I meant you!"

"No, I know. I don't mean any disrespect. Just checking because silver spoons don't taste good to me and never have, and I don't want to give that image off to you or anyone." I need him to know I'm not one of them.

He says very quietly, "Samantha, I don't mind talking about my life and I really don't mind talking about it with you. It's good, we're good, okay?"

I smile, "Ok."

"So enough about me!" He says happily, "Tell me about you."

"Two steak and cheese sandwiches," Frankie says as he delivers our sandwiches and looks to Hayden, "Hayden, how did it go the other day with Gerry? Did he come to your office to see you? I asked him and he said he would have you check him out. I just don't think he did. Gerry is an old mule who thinks he goes to the doctor every time he bellies up to the bar."

Hayden says, "Frankie, you know I can't tell you that! Patient doctor confidentiality," and he looks at me and winks and shoots at me, "That would hold up in court right?"

I shake my head smiling; he's a crapper and he knows it.

I like it, and him. He's cute in an annoying way.

I dive right into my sandwich because I'm starving, and this steak and cheese is delicious.

"Wow this is good!" And with a mouthful he says, "So tell me where you're from? Enough about me. Where did you grow up?"

My mouth is full and chewing furiously while holding a napkin to my lips, "Oh, me?" I chew mid-sentence, "Well I'm from here, the city. I grew up here. My parents went to college here in NY where they met. My dad is a professor at the community college and my mom does a lot for local charities."

Just then he starts to stand up, napkin in hand, and reaches his body halfway over the table and leans his face closer to mine.

What the hell is he doing? Oh, my shit, he is going to kiss me.

No, you can't kiss me, I have terrible breath, gosh no. I am screaming inside as his hand moves closer to me and just then I stand straight up, knocking over my glass and say, "I have to pee" and make a run for the bathroom.

Just like that. I bolt. I bolt from a kiss.

I slam the bathroom door shut sweating like an 8-year-old running in gym class and close the toilet seat and sit on it staring at the ceiling while my heart is beating so loud.

What the hell just happened?

He was going to kiss me; my mother's doctor was going to kiss me.

How can I go back out there!?

I move closer to the mirror and stare at myself, "Alright, Sam, what are you going to do now?"

Then I notice my mouth; I look closer to my face, then my mouth in the mirror and oh my god.

"No, please tell me this isn't happening."

Along the top of my lip is a large blob of mayonnaise smeared like a milk mustache; I look like an idiot. Do I not know how to eat!?

He wasn't about to kiss me; he was about to wipe this 'stache off my face.

You have got to be kidding me, can this get any more ridiculous?

I look up at the sky and address my higher power directly, "Oh yeah? Suddenly heaven has a funnies' section?"

I take a deep breath, wipe my mayo mustache off, and head straight back to the table like a champ.

"Hey, sorry about that. I really needed to use the ladies' room," I shrug and sit back down, "I'm also sorry about spilling my drink. Thank you for cleaning it up; I probably shouldn't have had a drink. I'm clumsy, by nature anyway. *Ok*. Where were we?"

He's taking it all in; he probably thinks I'm absolutely nuts. He isn't too far from the truth now, but I need to recover from my outburst.

"Well, you were telling me about your parents, but tell me about you," I have his full attention and he wants to know about me.

"Oh, yes, of course. I'm an only child, I grew up mostly around adults. I'm an attorney here in the city, I live alone with my cat. I'm an attorney and I like to work," I say quickly to wrap up the subject.

"Well, ok, Samantha Jenkins the attorney who has a cat and likes to work, what do you like to do for fun," He asks.

"For fun? I like to come home and watch Netflix to relax. I like to go to the park on my lunch breaks and people watch. Have you ever people-watched? New York is *by far* the best for watching people. It's a riot, at times. Sometimes, Dexter has lunch with me, and we laugh our butts off watching people, it's so entertaining," I am laughing just thinking about it and he is simply listening intently and watching me.

"Ok, so you people watch. And what other hobbies do you like?" he asks, tilting his head.

What is up with this guy, I'm not eighty years old, I don't have hobbies. He thinks I want to share more; I don't want to, and I won't.

It is not something I am comfortable with and in fact, I feel put on the spot.

"I don't, ok?" I say curtly.

He giggles, "Well, ok! So, Jenkins, what is something you want to do in life but never dared to yet? Like a bucket list item."

Jenkins? Ok, I'll take it, he likes to banter. Two can play that game.

"A bucket list item? I've never heard of that before. What would I like to do? Well, I think I want to learn how to ride a bike!" I share.

His eyes get big "WHAT?! You don't know how to ride a bike?!"

"No," I say, almost embarrassed. I know it's a weird thing to not learn in childhood, but I never really dared to.

If you ride a bike and fall, everyone sees. Over and over; fail, fail, fail.

I continue with, "I never really wanted to," but what I mean to say is I never dared to because I didn't want to fail, "But it's fine because there are buses and taxis and the subway, so I didn't need to."

It seemed incredibly hard as a kid, and I wasn't sure I could do it.

Suddenly his voice softens in a way that catches my attention and I listen intently.

"That's tough. Riding my bike as a child was some of the best days of my life. Me and my friends would ride without touching the handlebars; we raised our arms in the air going down the big hill in our town. We practiced night and day, found ways to do tricks. We rode our bikes to the stream and went fishing, down to the store and grabbed ourselves root beers and pretended they were real beer."

He chuckles, "We were little shits but also good boys. We rode anywhere and everywhere in our town, we were like a little pack," he says then takes a deep breath and continues.

"I guess those are my good old days."

He looks adorable as he shares this with me, lit up and alive. His eyes are wide and he's so passionate about his bikes and even more so about his friends.

There's a quiet pause as he reflects and then says with a laugh, "We thought we were the cool kids with our Huffy bikes."

He would make a good dad, I think to myself, *maybe even as good as my own father.*

He breaks my thoughts and adds, "Despite everything that happened in my childhood, riding on my bike I felt like I was on top of the world."

He looks at me and says, "You know what, Jenkins? You have to try it. You have nothing to lose, add it to your bucket list! This is New York City; we all ride bikes. I'll teach you!"

I laugh at his excitement, "Ok, how can I not, with you asking me like that!"

I giggle because he's something else.

I glance at my phone and yikes it's already 10pm.

"I need to go home, it's late and I haven't fed my cat," I look at him and say again, "Thank you so much for the evening. It really was nice." I flip open my wallet and start to pull out my debit card.

"No, please, it's on me! I body slammed you and this is my restitution," he says and smiles.

"Ok, Dr. Bryant, deal. I accept this payment. Seriously, though, thank you," I smile back at him, "I'll see you at the hospital?"

I extend my hand and awkwardly go to shake his because I don't really know what else to do and this seems fitting.

"Bye, Jenkins."

I walk out of the bar and the warm breeze hits my face and feels so good; *I feel good.*

This guy is something else.

"Bye, Jenkins," I say out loud, repeating him.

Even if we're just friends, this guy has a way of injecting life into me, he is so passionate about everything he takes an interest in.

He also has a beautiful smile that lights up everything around him.

He is *so* positive.

How can someone withstand such tragedy and have so much happiness and passion for life?

I'm not sure but it's contagious; it has me wanting to jump into life.

MAybe this is my next step in feeling alive.

Chapter 11

I smiled during my entire drive home last night; I feel good, refreshed.

When my head hits my pillow, I sleep more soundly than I have in weeks and I definitely needed it last night.

I needed an escape from the chaos and Hayden is a good guy to have around, even as a friend.

I'm content as I lay in bed this morning with Leroy curled on a ball near my head.

"Mm," I stretch my arms and legs and get my buns out of bed, feeling energized.

It's going to be an amazing day.

Let's get something straight; I have never been a daring person.

I'm confident in how I communicate in the office against prosecutors, and I've always stood my ground.

I always and I mean *always* scheduled *everything*; I love a checklist and crossing everything on that sucker off.

While some would call me a routine type of person, I call myself a creature of habit.

But this morning? This morning feels different.

To hell with my schedule. I may not be able to ride a bike, but this girl is about to feel just as daring.

But first, forget work. I reach over to my phone on my nightstand and text Dexter.

Dex, I am not going to attend this morning's debriefing; I have a laundry list of to do's and maybe even a couple ta-das, but I have to be at the hospital by 10 at the very latest. I'm sorry to bail but cover for me and we can have breakfast tomorrow morning, ok?

Bring your laptop, we'll go over work then. Meet me at the hospital cafe at 8! Love you and miss you more than you know!

Dexter responds immediately.

Hey, fancy girl. Yea work is boring without you but don't worry about things here, I totally have it. I am far more interested in knowing about your ta-das, sweetie. You must fill me in, why are you talking like that? See you tomorrow!

Oh gosh, he is so nosy even if he's right, something is up.

I jump out of bed, walk to my closet, and scan over my color-coded outfits.

This is my mother's influence; organization was drilled into me over the years.

I split the clothes right down the middle with both hands pushing the hangers to both sides to reveal the shelves behind it where I stash the clothes I feel most comfortable in. I grab my patchwork jeans and a flannel shirt, and throw them on, roll each pant leg up one turn, throw on my Chucks and, because it's almost winter, grab my knitted sweater to guard against the chill in the air.

I fill Leroy's dish and tell him, "Today's going to be another long day, guy, I need you to be patient with me. Mother needs us and these large bowls of food and water must last you at least till supper. No snacking."

He twirls around my ankles rubbing himself against my legs; he knows the drill. I stoop down to his level and rub my face against him as he presses against me.

"Love you, my man. Be good!"

I grab my baseball cap and pull my ponytail through the hole, grab my wallet, and take a pause because I'm about to do something my heart has wanted to do for *years*.

My first stop is the convenience store. I grabbed the items I always need and what *she* will need; Chapstick, gum, makeup remover, nail polish remover, and because soft hands are important, hand cream.

My next stop is the department store, which is about to be a challenge.

My excitement has me moving quickly; I'm zipping along, my pulse racing.

Hayden would be concerned if he could feel it, but this is a great galloping pulse.

I'm excited because I feel sneaky, spontaneous, and in charge.

I enter the women's section at a department store I rarely frequent because my leisure clothes have always been fine, and my professional clothes come to me directly from a subscription box based in California. Easy peasy. I pay my monthly fee and she outfits me, head to toe, for work.

I go from rack to rack trying to stay on my schedule, pulling out pair after pair of jeans.

Mom jeans, way-too-low teeny bopper jeans. Elastic waist jeans. Shoot me if I ever think wearing jeans like these are ok.

Lord, this is a challenge, and how these styles can be worn is beyond me.

I sort through sweaters, shirts, sweatshirts, cardigans until out of the corner of my eye I spot a rack of overalls. Now these are adorable, and totally something I would wear. They have yellow and red bandana-colored patches on the knees and on the front pocket, a little daisy patch with a ladybug on it.

These are cute.

Yep, I think, and swing them over my arm.

Right next to it are ribbed fitted sweaters, a cute red one that matches a couple of the patches on the overalls. *Perfect!*

Plus, hospitals are chilly, and mother needed to be warm; she is so frail and cold in her recovery, always wrapped up and still shivering.

This will be comfy and cozy for her.

I walk across the street over to the shoe store; I come *here* a lot.

I'm a wee bit addicted to comfy shoes, comfy slippers, comfy flip-flops. But who keeps track when you live alone?

I see a new color of Chuck's in a bright teal and grab them for myself, then rethink and grab the yellow instead.

Focus, Sam, focus!

My phone starts to ring, and I pull it out of my back pocket; it's my dad calling.

"Hey Dad!!" I answer.

"Hello, kiddo. I haven't touched base with you in days. We keep missing each other at the hospital and wanted to check on you before I head into class."

I smile. I love this man; he is such a great dad. Big shoes for any man to fill.

"Well, Dad, I am doing some light shopping this morning, then heading to the hospital," I share, haltingly, feeling shy suddenly.

"Light shopping? Sammy, since when have you been a shopper? What are you *really* doing? And don't fall behind at work. If you need to switch shifts with me, I'll fill in on mornings and have Matt cover class for me a few times."

"Dad, really, I'm fine. Dexter works directly with the clients, and I communicate with him on the hour, I'm fine. Oh gosh, dad, I'm losing reception," I pull the phone from my face.

"Dad, are you still there? I can't hear you," I say, knowing full well he can hear me.

I hear him say faintly, "Yeah, I can kind of hear you, Sam. Ok, sounds like you're in a bad area. Call me later, and I love you."

'What dad? I think you said I love you. Love you too. Bye." I press end because I cannot have him getting any more curious about my plans. I love him but he knows when I'm full of it.

So, with my arms full of shopping bags, I throw them in the passenger seat of my Bug, throw it into gear and head toward the hospital where mom is about to have a side of fun she never knew she needed.

With all three bags in my arms cutting off my blood flow, I wait while the elevator doors slide open to the oncology ward. Passing by the nurse's station, I make eye contact with our night nurse, wink, smirk, and say, "Give me an hour with her."

She presses her lips together, squints her eyes, and cocks her head and raises her eyebrows.

She knows I'm up to something and says, "Great timing. Her roommate has therapy this morning."

And then winks back.

I feel a mischievous in me that is almost palpable to the people around me, a bounce in my step that has me feeling like I can do anything, and an unfamiliar feeling for my mother that I'm finally open to.

I go to her door and say, "Knock, knock" with a sing-sing tone of voice.

"Hello?" I hear her faint voice from the corner of the room, her voice that was so strong only a few months ago.

I walk in and peek around the corner past the curtain to look at her.

"Hi mom! Want some company?" I wait for her to answer before stepping in.

"Yes, of course," she clears her throat carefully, "I just finished breakfast. I slept like a baby last night so I think today I should be able to make some phone calls…"

I walk in and she starts in surprise, "Samantha, why on God's green Earth are you dressed like that?!"

Her expression is almost one of disgust.

Be strong Sam, be strong.

"Well, I have something else planned for us this morning that isn't phone calls," I tell her with a confidence so unfamiliar to her that she stills and doesn't answer, but maintains eye contact with me, a curious look on her face.

I have her attention, although she still says nothing, and I completely ignore her question about my clothing.

Like Kramer walking into a room on Seinfeld, I throw the hospital privacy curtain back and blow in like a breath of fresh air, then place the bags on the floor near her bed.

Her eyes follow me as I close the door and move the IV stand, then position myself to face her; I take both her hands in mine, look up to her face and say, "Mother. You have spent the last nearly 30 years raising a family. You have made sure you crossed every "T" and dotted every "I" never thinking about yourself, and I have spent my entire life wanting to be the woman you are. You've made sure I always knew how to conduct myself and corrected any and everything I needed to correct. You do everything so effortlessly and never hesitate to give to others. You have always made sure I said, did, wore, and became everything I needed to be, and I love how much you want greatness from and for me. Thank you, mother."

She stays silent.

This is uncomfortable for us both, because it's a conversation I was raised to avoid even if they're words I need to say.

We've left phrases like "thank you" and "I love you" unspoken but this isn't the time for things being left unsaid.

"Today I want to take care of you, Mother. You have been here day after day, not able to do anything aside from worry or wait for the nurses or doctors. Today, we are playing by my rules. It may be uncomfortable, and you may not want to do it again after, but it means a lot to me. That is if…. if you let me spend the morning doing what I want to do with you."

There is complete silence.

"Mother, that was a question," I say, urging her to participate.

"Samantha, you know very well I cannot leave the hospital because I am in no condition to do so, according to the doctor. I'm attached to all these wires and who knows what tests they will be doing today and I…" she's resisting but I can hear in her voice that I'm about to wear her down.

"Mom. Stop." I hold her hand and gently squeeze to reassure her, "Trust me. Trust that I will take care of you today, right here, and we aren't going anywhere."

She inhales and then exhales; she pulls herself up from the pillows propping her up, and says, "Well, fine then. What do you need me to do?"

I jump into immediate action before she can change her mind.

I grab my phone and hit play on my favorite playlist called Free to Be Me and the first song kicks it off perfectly; The Proclaimers *I'm Gonna Be (500 miles)*.

I sing along and mom looks on with an eyebrow raised as she listens to me sing for the first time since elementary school events.

I sing away loud and while I grab the bag with the nail polish remover and remove my mother's nail polish, the same color she's been wearing as long as I can remember.

Her hands are stiff as a board, her face is white as a ghost as she wonders what the hell I'm doing.

She can't get a word in because I'm singing away.

I move to the other side of the bed and take the polish off her other hand, and, for a quick second, I pause. Her hands look beautiful and unadorned. I can see her nail beds, her long, elegant fingers.

This is fun, yes, but she just became more beautiful to me in a way that I can't explain.

I sense that she's extremely uncomfortable; I gently touch mothers chin and guide her face to look at me.

"Mother, this is going to be hard but please. Trust me."

She still says nothing, and I watch the rise and fall of each breath in her chest as the beeping of her machines behind her continue to report her vitals.

I grab the makeup remover because, to me, this part is personal; I've never for the life of me seen my mother without makeup and because she always has input when I wear makeup of my own.

I take the little make up pads and slowly and carefully begin to swipe her makeup from her forehead working my way down to her cheeks, over her beautiful high cheekbones that I wish she had passed down to me.

I move around almost like a facial and she closes her eyes, I'm not sure if she has them closed because she's enjoying it, or she can't stand to see herself without makeup- I'm guessing it's the latter because I know I've never seen her without it.

The next song begins to kick on and the irony makes me chuckle to myself, *Little Miss Can't Be Wrong* by the Spin Doctors and it's a good thing her eyes are closed because I can't help but smile.

She peeks through one eye and catches me grinning; as I wipe her lipstick off, I swear I see her grinning back.

I sit back and take in the sight of my mom without makeup.

Why hadn't she thought of this before?

What she looks like when her natural beauty is allowed to shine is so different.

I look so much like her.

I am so in love with this moment; this is going to my head but right now I'm unstoppable.

I buzz around the room and tend to my mother's frail body, giving her a day to remember, I hope.

"Ok mother. Hair time."

"No, absolutely *not*," she says with more defiance than I expected from her.

"Yowzah, mom! But too bad. Today's my day," I say with a smile.

She shakes her head either in annoyance or frustration, but she doesn't stand a chance; I possess an inner strength she hasn't seen before.

Look at that, I think to myself, Hayden's "yowzah" worked! I smile to myself when I think of him.

As the next song comes on, *Safety Dance*, I begin to sing like I'm alone in my car; it's a concert and I am more than a little dramatic.

This is *not* a side of me she's met or seen before.

I begin to brush her long brown hair, knotted from being bedridden and I try very hard to be gentle; I should have done this days ago. I brush slowly, untangling the knots with my fingers.

I can almost feel her brushing my hair when I was little, sitting in her chair in front of the full-length mirror in her bedroom.

Oh, how our roles have reversed.

Separating her hair strand from strand so as not to hurt her, I untangle her hair; over the years it's grown coarse. I notice that elderly people's hair, their texture, almost feels tired.

I never noticed how her hair has become as weathered as her hands; her age is becoming real to me right now.

I take her hair and split it right down the middle of the back of her head and on one side begin to braid her hair.

This feels like deja vu.

When I was little I used to watch her "programs" aka her tv shows, with her.

One of them was *Little House on the Prairie* and the mother would braid her hair before bed; it made me wonder what my mother would look like with braids. Or even if maybe she, too, went to bed with her hair braided in secret. I love thinking about that even more so at this moment.

I braid both sides of her hair and when a new song kicks on I see mom's right foot moving to the beat of the music.

I'm dying laughing because I never would have thought she knew this song but she sure as heck knows the beat.

I start singing as I finish braiding her right side.

And no, I don't want no scrub; a scrub is a guy that can't get no love from me.

Then, in that moment, mother opens her eyes and does something I would never in my wildest dreams imagine her doing; she finishes the chorus along with me, knowing every word perfectly.

I start laughing and I cannot for the life of me stop, I literally have tears rolling down my cheeks and when I look at her, she's smiling. Her smile is so sweet. At this moment she looks and feels different.

She says very confidently and with a little bit of humor, "Look. I might be a hard ass, but I wasn't born yesterday. You know I can sing too, Samantha."

I have nothing to say to that, I'm stunned.

Happily stunned.

I have a mother that I've never known lurking inside the one I have always struggled to connect with.

"Well, in that case mother," I say and begin yanking the clothes of their bags.

I spend the next ten minutes changing my mother out of her silk pajamas, being careful of her drainage bags and all her tubes, and she lets me.

I change her into the overalls and shirt I bought her earlier this morning.

She tries so hard to be expressionless, but her body is tapping to the music, and she's smiling; my mother is loving this, and I'm finding a new way to love *her*.

To love us.

"Ok. So, now we're going for a little walk around the nurse's station to stretch, but, before we do, you need shoes. Hold on. . ."

I forward my playlist to Cindy Lauper's *True Colors* and take out her new yellow shoes and place them on her feet.

I look up as I tie them and see tears rolling down her face.

When I'm done, I sit next to her and use a tissue to wipe her tears. I reach into my pocket, hold her by the chin and turn her face toward mine and put ChapStick on her very dry lips.

"Mother, it goes like this," and put her ChapStick on in the way that looks best for her, the way she taught me.

I lean in and whisper in her ear, "I love you, mom."

And then, she places her head on my shoulder and quietly says, "You are the best thing that I have ever made. Thank you for knowing what I need and for giving it to me."

I feel the heaviness of her head on my shoulder, and can feel the heaviness of her heart, as well.

I will never forget this moment; I'm enjoying it and, sooner than later, I will want desperately to be able to go back to it when it's just out of reach.

I lift her by her arms, steadily, while grabbing her IV pole, detach her blood pressure cuff and pulse/ox monitor, and we walk out of the room slowly to walk around the ward.

We pass many other patients who are doing the same even in hospital gowns.

One older lady tells her husband as they walk by, "Now look at them. Aren't they just cute as a button." I look at my mother's face and she smiles but also can't resist rolling her eyes. I laugh out loud. And say, "It's fine. We're both cute as buttons."

While passing the nurse's station I am not sure who is beaming more, us or the staff, but every nurse grins at us and even a few tear up as they watch us together.

"Good morning, Jenkins Ladies! You both look beautiful, today," They call as we walk by.

She has never been one to accept this but this time she says, "Thank you, ladies. Thank you so much. I get it from my daughter."

We walk the roundabout until we make it back to her room.

Once we get back to the room, she's exhausted, today is a lot and I can see it in her face; I lay her gently back into her bed.

She leans with a gentle smile, almost a look of feeling whole, complete.

"Mother, I'll let you rest. But I hope you loved this morning," I say, tucking the blankets around her.

"No. Don't go," She scoots over a tad and says, "Come lay down with me."

I start to object because she looks so feeble, tired. Probably from our active morning. I notice a pale-yellow tint to her skin, almost like jaundice.

It must be the lighting in this room.

"Mother, I..." but she takes her finger and holds it over her mouth and says, "Shhh. Let's rest."

I take our shoes off, grab the lotion I purchased and put a little on my hands; I lay with my mother and massage the cream into her hands.

As I do this, it is peacefully quiet. My hands begin to massage slower; I'm sleepy, too.

We close our eyes and we both nod off to sleep together.

Me, lying beside my frail mother, my mother holding my hands while we rest.

This is a feeling like no other, a feeling that pulls my mind back to last night with Hayden.

He triggered a piece of me that was unknown to so many and shared with so few.

He makes me want to be more.

I feel my breathing in sync with my mother's pulse, and we hold hands as we fall asleep, lulled by her heartbeat the way I was as a child.

Chapter 12

Walter Jenkins knew he needed to get to the hospital to relieve his daughter.

She had taken plenty of time off work this past week to be with his wife, her mother, and he imagined she could use a breather and he only had classes till noon today.

He decided, at the last minute, to cancel an afternoon class, a decision that was as rare as Walter calling in sick.

He had to clean up before going to the hospital. A quick stop at home, grab a bite of last night's dinner, and he would be at his wife's side by 1:30pm. This would allow his daughter, Samantha, to either go to the office or go home to rest and unwind.

Plus, he missed Eleanor; she was his rock. His place beside her always felt like home.

Walter rode his bicycle to work almost every day because it gave him almost five miles of exercise and fresh air when he did.

He had done this for years; being healthy was always important to Ellie, the nickname he shortened Eleanor to.

But today, it was gloomy out and if Ellie were home, she would have him drive into work to stay safe.

As he pulled up to the house, just like that, there was a complete downpour. He looked up, smiled, and said out loud, "For an old coot, I'm not too bad at making decisions without my wife."

He shook his head and rode through the gates and up the driveway to the house; Ellie would have giggled at this.

He was always one to respect his wife, she was the light of his life.

They had been married for almost 40 years, since college, and he still had a soft spot for her tender side, as rarely as it was shown to the world.

Ellie was feisty.

This is what attracted him to her in the first place. He fell in love with her feisty side but soft side and to this day she made him weak in his knees.

Since her diagnosis, he was trying too hard to convince himself that she would champion through her illness and be back to normal in no time, but deep down he knew that her firing squad days may be over. He had spent 40 years needing this beautiful woman in every aspect of this life. He had always felt that she made him a better man.

She was the one, this time, who needed Walter; her and their daughter.

Samantha was a lot like her dad in many ways but she was strong like her mom, too, and was doing an excellent job of being there for the both of them.

Walter got lost in his thoughts, sitting on the bed changing his socks and shoes, loosening his necktie, and putting on Ellie's favorite sweater that she loved for him to wear.

He looked around.

The bedroom felt empty these days but still smelled like his wife.

Every night since Ellie had been in the hospital going to bed was hard; sure, he called before bed to say good night and hear her voice, but he longed for her to be next to him reading by her little bedtime book light.

During last night's call, she whispered, "I miss you". These days his own hearing was lagging, but he heard just enough to know his Ellie loved and needed him.

He looked up and saw that Ellie's office door was unlatched and slightly open; she had probably left it open a bit.

He got up and he closed the door, then paused, he opened the door again and stepped into the room.

He squinted his eyes against the light from the window in the back, saw the haze in the air, inhaled.

He looked around this room that was off limits to everyone.

He had always respected Ellie's wishes, even if he never fully agreed with them but deep down in his heart, he knew this room would be something he would one day be forced to explain.

He knew this and every day he struggled with the thought; he quickly closed the door and made sure it was tightly latched.

It was time to go see his bride, he thought.

Walter jumped in his car and headed to visit Eleanor at the hospital where she had been for far too long, according to his heart.

*   *   *   *   *

    *   *

As Walter exited the elevator on the ward where his wife was staying, he walked slowly by each patient's room.

He always had the urge to glance into each one while making the trek down the corridor to Ellie's room.

Some had patients that never seemed to have visitors. He wondered if they didn't have children or maybe their children lived far away. It must be a terrible, heart-wrenching loneliness for these patients.

Walter found he had a lump in his throat knowing full well that these patients could very well pass away alone.

Samantha was the greatest gift that he and Ellie shared.

Not only was parenting Samantha great but now that she was an adult her friendship with her parents, and her company gave them something to look forward to as they grew older together.

Every day when he looked at his wife, he fell more in love with her, even after all these years.

Ellie worked hard all of Samantha's life and was hands-on with their daughter's education and every other aspect of her development; there was nothing passive about Eleanor's involvement with the day-to-day growth of her family.

He knows, deep down, it was Ellie's way of keeping their daughter close to home. Sammy had always attended local private schools here in the city when most of her friends' children were being sent across the country and abroad to various boarding schools.

Once college came, Ellie's father, Sam's grandfather, George, was always a large benefactor for colleges in the city and his granddaughter, Samantha's, number one school choice was not only George's alma mater, but a college he gave a large sum of money annually to for their science department.

Having her close-by, these days, was a gift in the care of Eleanor.

As he approached the doorway to her room, a nurse walked toward Walter, her finger against her lips.

"Shhh. They have been sleeping for over an hour," she told him.

He was confused.

Who has been sleeping, he wondered, *They?*

He started to quietly walk into the room, not sure what he was about to find; maybe the nurse meant Ellie and her roommate were sleeping.

He opened the door and could tell someone was sitting in the chair under the TV at the end of her bed; as he drew closer, he noticed it was Dr. Bryant sitting there.

Dr. Hayden Bryant, Ellie's surgeon. His heart stopped. Was something wrong?

Dr. Bryant looked up and saw Walter coming in and immediately got up and nodded his head to talk in the hallway.

This time Walter could feel the blood drain to his feet; something was wrong.

"Dr. Bryant. Is there something wrong?" Walter asked and Hayden could tell that Walter was worried.

'No, Walter. Don't worry. The ladies have been resting and when I went to check on Mrs. Jenkins I took a second to sit and chart my notes. Seems they both had quite a morning." Hayden smiled and continued, "The nurses told me there was music coming from her room and Samantha had her Mom walking around…" he paused, "Although not in hospital attire."

Walter was confused; not in her hospital attire?

What was he talking about? Now he was more confused than his wife's roommate, he thought to himself.

"Ok, Doc. You got me," Walter started to say but Hayden grabbed Walter's arm carefully and quieted him with a finger to his lips, then brought Walter in the room and gently pulled the curtain back.

Walter's heart came right back up from his feet and into his throat.

The two most important women in his life, the women he loved more than life itself.

The two women who, on the outside were so very much the same, and on the inside were more alike than either of them knew.

His whole world was lying in a hospital bed asleep and holding each other.

The world couldn't have looked more beautiful to Walter than this moment.

Walter looked at Hayden and the men locked eyes; Hayden watched Walter's eyes fill up with tears.

All Hayden could manage to say was, "I know."

Walter responded without taking his eyes off his wife and daughter, "If you only knew..."

Hayden decided to give this man time with his family and quietly excused himself.

As he walked out he couldn't help but feel choked up, himself. *This right here*, he thought to himself, *is why I practice medicine*. It's *what makes me want more.*

And this right here was what he wanted for a family of his own.

Dr. Bryant tries wiping away the thought of the ladies sleeping so soundly, so beautifully, and makes himself jump on the computer at the nurse's station to get his mind back to work. He needs to check Eleanor Jenkins' most recent lab and MRI results since her surgery.

He knows thinking of Samantha wasn't doing any good and he is completely out of line for doing so.

There just is something about her, something that feels right.

Looking at Sam with her family, it is obvious how much life she brought to her mother this morning.

But last night; last night she did what nobody had ever done to Hayden.

She woke up a piece of himself that he hadn't quite been open to, that had been sleeping since he was a little boy.

She does something to him that he hasn't been able to shake since that night at Sully's.

She is easy to be with and there was *just* something about her.

Her giggle, the way she looks at him, and her odd way of flirting.

Or maybe she wasn't flirting. He thinks.

He really wasn't sure, but he *was* sure he shouldn't even be thinking of this girl.

Right now, he has to focus on work.

Oddly enough, that means the same thing because he looks at the results twice and his own heart drops at what he is seeing on the computer.

This did not look good.

He has to consult with Dr. Piper Immediately before he says anything, but Hayden's head drops at the thought of delivering this news.

He was about to break this family.

Chapter 13

In the last week and a half since her surgery, when mother rests, I rest, I take advantage of the quiet where I can.

I'm trying hard to get into the habit of creating me-time.

But I sit here with yesterday at the forefront in my heart and can't help but see that there is a part of me feeling alive, a part of me that I want to make public. It inspires me.

Hayden has turned on a light in me that I didn't recognize, a light that I not only need but want; I have a hunger for me that leaves me wanting more.

Since coming home from mom's room at the hospital, I haven't been able to stop drawing.

Nonstop sketching and painting, pouring out of me like a waterfall.

When I woke up yesterday from my nap with mom, I was ready to sketch, and I couldn't get home to my apartment fast enough. I curled up on my chaise right near my balcony with my calming classical music blasting in my air pods. This is where the sun lit my apartment the best, bright and warm and cozy.

It's where most of my canvases come to life.

The minute I picked up my pencil, I lost track of the time and for what seemed like light years, I drew, and I drew.

I started working on the canvas of my "little couple" on the swings; my hands wouldn't, couldn't stop sketching.

I kept changing pencil colors, adding shades to each line.

I was focused and lost in the moment.

My mind imagining this couple I was sketching.

What are their names?

How many children would they have had together?

How many babies had they held together?

How did they meet?

What made them connect and stay in love, forever?

I stopped and took a breath and stared at my progress.

I breathed in and exhaled burying their story behind the strokes of my pencil.

What could or would I call this piece of work?

This one was different; this one seemed deeper than others I had painted or sketched.

Their bodies, the sky behind them, even the old rustic metal poles the swings swung from, everything, was coming together.

It started to create a life.

Since I had been at the hospital all week I think I've sketched almost every part of this hospital.

I had drawings of the waiting room with the afternoon sunlight pouring through the window, the water fountain in the outside community picnic area with two birds bathing together in it.

I sketched all week long but the last two days since starting this one, it's different, changing; I'm becoming a different artist.

I have a different flavor of passion in my pallet and goals, in this piece, I'd never thought of before.

This painting has started to mean more to me.

My mind knows these two people or maybe it's even that I want to have what I imagine they have.

I tend to do that when I'm sitting outside my office building at lunch while I people-watch; I give people stories.

Some are romantic stories while others are funny ones but all of them connect me to them.

With people watching, I almost believe what I'm thinking is true because of how they act, the way they walk, and the way they talk to others. I piece their lives together and then turn it into a painting.

Everyone has a story. But I think, maybe, sometimes I am so caught up in other storylines that I'm forgetting to make a story and a life of my own.

The last couple of weeks, I've found myself daydreaming about building more than just court cases, creating more than just paintings.

I need to start finding out what fills my cup.

Do I know I haven't ever put in the time or energy to think about this aspect of my life with any depth; when you're busy it's kind of an easy subject to avoid.

But in hindsight, at this moment, on paper, I have a degree and a cat and that was always enough for me. I was comfortable, content, and it worked.

Since the other night at Sully's, with Hayden, though I know I need more.

I need to have a real, whole, rich life and that evening woke up a desire for that that I never knew existed, a feeling of wanting more.

There was something about Dr. Hayden Bryant that made me inhale, close my eyes, tilt my head back, and feel alive, which is a feeling that I'm not sure how to re-invent without him.

This morning, I'm meeting Dexter for breakfast at the hospital; we have files to go over, and other things I cannot wait to discuss with him that are more fun than work.

Dexter, my secret keeper, will love to hear what's been going on.

As I'm walking past the courtyard I had spent many days of the last week in, it is starting to become so familiar, especially the smell but this is my new norm.

Even the nurses know me.

I often escape to the courtyard and the nurses and even some patients come up behind me where I sit on the bench and watch me while Mother is in therapy.

I feel their stares over my shoulder as I draw, the old nurses especially because they got closer for a better look and asked a lot of questions.

Moments like that make me remember when I was in law school and would go to central park to study but ended up pulling out my pad and drawing; it was mostly elderly people who stopped to strike up conversations.

They're lonely, sure, but honestly, it filled me with my own kind of inspiration.

It was what I did; I drew.

It became how I let my feelings out and it led to self-care for that little piece of me that longs to be accepted and myself.

Having strangers view my drawings and paintings, see my work separately from me, is comfortable and comforting.

I like it this way.

 It carries no expectations, no judgment. They see past me and into my work and it feels safe.

But I am tired of eating alone, tired of watching movies alone.

I am tired of *being* alone.

I am tired.

Dad called me last night.

Mother was in and out of sleep, exhausted from our morning. She finally gave in and took her meds, which gives us all hope that she'll sleep and heal. He told me he hoped she would sleep through the night, and he thanked me for helping and promised to be there this afternoon.

The sun is coming up, the air is chilly, and my belly is reminding me it's time to eat.

Having breakfast with Dexter is exactly what I need.

It's the top of breakfast hour and going in, I hear the bustle of the breakfast crew; dishes clanking, silverware rattling. There is me and a couple more people in line waiting for the buffet to open.

"Excuse me, ma'am," I hear someone say behind me then I feel a tap on my shoulder.

It's mom's nurse, Charlene.

"Oh, hello, Charlene! I'm so sorry, I didn't realize you were talking to me," I say to this young woman who has helped mom since she checked her in.

"I'm not sure if y'all remember me but I'm your mother's nurse on the third floor," she says in the most Southern accent I've heard since visiting mom's family in Georgia as a child.

"Yes, I remember you. How are you?" I ask, smiling pleasantly at her blonde hair all tied up in a messy bun at the top of her head.

"I'm good, I'm on break and forgot my breakfast at home so I thought I'd get myself down to breakfast and grab something to fill my tummy. It's fixin' to be a long morning with this double shift, we have a full house." She says matter-of-factly.

"Oh gosh that's hard. I could never do what you do. I mean, my mother isn't the easiest to deal with, and I know you've already taken a beating," I smile and by way of telling her that I get it.

"Oh, my heavens, *no*! She's great. Feisty, but great! She takes no crud from anyone and honestly, if we could all be like that, I'm certain we could live and work in this place a whole lot easier. But bless her heart, she speaks highly of you. Her sweet side comes out when she speaks of her family."

Oh gosh this can't be good, I think to myself and brace myself.

"Oh, she does, does she? I don't even want to know what she's told you, but only believe half of what she shares. The other half is what she wants to be true, not necessarily what I've done," I wink at her hoping she gets me.

"Oh Darlin', after yesterday with you, she's been sweet as pie! Even your dad spent the night with us," she winks and adds quietly and nudges me, "The day nurse told me what you did with your mama."

There's an awkward silence; I'm not sure how to respond.

"So, I know this is straightforward and totally tell me if you cannot. But I'm on the committee to the Annual Auction Fundraiser for the oncology ward and I have seen you doodling on your pad of paper and it's good." She says. Her peppiness is a lot to take in, but *doodling*?

I want to tell her I haven't doodled since I was seven.

"Well, thank you. It's something I do to pass the time with. Thank you.. But I…." I say and she cuts me off.

"Would you consider doing something or donating something you drew or painted for the annual auction? Finding items for this auction has been like herding cats. We have items being auctioned off, but your work could help raise money for the unit."

Yikes. I feel cornered because this feels very public. Not many people know I even own a sketch pad.

I gulp hard and say, "I mean, I don't see why not? I don't know if you would get a bid, but I wouldn't mind at all," I lower my voice and ask hesitantly, "Could I do it as an anonymous donation?"

She quickly answers and is too loud when she does, "Why, of course! I can add it to the list as an anonymous donation. Sure thing, sweetheart! I can do that!"

She is super excited, which makes me chuckle but I'm thinking this won't be as anonymous as I hoped. She *is* adorable and why the heck not, right?

I say, "Well, ok, then it's a deal. I will let you know when I complete it. Can you give me a couple days?" I ask hesitantly.

"Sure, I can!" She says with so much excitement that I take it to mean she doesn't have a great deal of donated items.

"I can see if my law firm wants to donate anything, as well." I suggest.

"Good gravy. Look at you! That would be awfully kind of you!" she answers, her face lighting up.

"Well, good, then I will see you on the ward. And, again, can we keep the auction between you and me?"

She pauses and almost like she understands "Oh, yes, of course. Bless your heart!" and she winks and starts toward the buffet to get something for her breakfast.

I grin.

Southern people are interesting to me, and I could listen to their accents all the time.

It sounds happy and fancy, with some style to it. It's almost like the South, in and of itself, is an entirely different country south of the Carolinas, a fancier part of the US. The part my mom is from.

I fill my plate and head over to the glass wall that overlooks the picnic area and pull out my phone to pass the time; I put my earbuds in and turn on Hulu to catch the local news until Dexter arrives.

I haven't been able to watch TV in weeks; not that I was ever a TV person, but I loved binging a series or two or maybe seven on a day when the mood strikes.

I set my phone on its stand and eat the scrambled eggs that I piled onto my plate, way more than I can eat. My eyes are always bigger than my stomach but I'm not sure what I'm doing for lunch. Plus, I'm starving. I haven't had normal meals in quite a few days.

Then, I feel hands on my shoulders, and I nearly jump out of my skin. I whip my head around, scared to death.

"Holy *shit,* Dexter, you scared the hell out of me!"

"Girl, settle down, it's not like you didn't know I was coming. Unless you want to cancel on me *again*!" He looks at my plate "But it looks like you have breakfast, lunch, and dinner covered," He laughs as he sits across from me, and throws his satchel on the table.

He's a stinker because I'm usually better at eating but now he looks at my breakfast plate like I'm eating for a team.

I laugh, "Yeah, my eyes are bigger than my stomach."

He leaves and comes back with a fork, "Guess you have enough for me," and he waves his hand to himself and starts to eat from my plate.

I get right down to business and say, "So, what's up? How's the office? I haven't really been able to check the google doc we share to catch up."

He rolls his eyes, waves his hand, and says, "Oh, girl. I'm not here to talk about work. It's totally fine; same shit, different day. Nothing I can't handle. We're doing *fine*, Sam. Why don't you tell me what's going on with *you*." He holds the vowel sound on the "you".

He's being nosy and he's being Dexter, and Dexter is such a good guy. He is my comfort zone, and he understands me.

"Oh, before you start," he says, not giving me a chance to answer, "Remember that painting at the last gallery exhibit that you sold? Well, I stopped by the gallery, and you know that buyer from about a month ago. Well, he came back looking for more paintings you may have in stock!"

Dexter was talking fast and animated.

"He was totally into your style. He said he was going to come back for the next show. So, I'm totally hoping you can be there if your mother is doing better!" He says and winks at me.

"He came back, huh?" I shrug my shoulders. I barely remember him, but I do remember he was cocky and snarky.

"Well, that's cool…right? Did he tell you his name? Because he was kind of a jerk that night and I met him for maybe two seconds." I pause and then continue, "But he came back looking again? Mister money bags, I guess."

Dexter gives me a dirty look and sits back. "Maybe he likes your work. Gosh, Sam. *Really*?"

He stops and looks at me, "What's your problem? You ok? You're acting weird."

"Yeah, just a lot to digest lately. Being here" I wave my hand around to indicate everything around me, "It is starting to feel stifling. Mother is so weak. The Doctors are saying it's normal and it will take time for her to regain her strength. But, I mean, we had a great morning yesterday. It was fun."

I tell him all about it and get excited about it all over again thinking about our day together.

"Literally, Dexter, I'm sitting and watching her day in and day out. But then I woke up and got her out of bed and we had a great time. She let me dress her up in overalls, and we listened to music. We …"

He cuts me off and reaches over to place his hand over mine and says, "She is on some heavy drugs, huh?"

I burst out laughing, and I mean *loud*. I am dying, giggling uncontrollably.

He thinks the only way we could or would do this is mother on drugs; I am doubled over laughing, so hard and hysterically even though I know it isn't that funny.

Dexter looks around and demands, "Sam. Stop."

But I can't stop, I'm cackling, and tears are rolling down my face.

He covers his mouth with one hand, he is starting to crack up laughing because I am laughing.

Together we are laughing with tears rolling down our faces; I'm not sure what he's releasing but this laugh was freeing every ounce of stress I've built up over the last week and a half, every ounce of happiness I managed to collect in the last day and a half.

Without realizing it we have company, someone standing at our table staring down at us.

I am not sure how long we laugh while he stands there, but clearly longer than we think.

He clears his throat to make his presence known and I look up.

"Oh! Hayden…I mean… Dr. Bryant." I stood quickly, "Hi!"

I extend my hand out for a shake and he looks down at it for so long that I pull it away.

Should I have done that? Too formal? I wonder.

I was scrambling nervously and turned to Dexter, "Hi. Dexter, this is my mother's doctor, Dr. Bryant. Dr. Bryant, this is my best friend and paralegal, Dexter."

Dexter looks at him and stands up and Hayden looks back at him; they're both visibly uncomfortable.

It's quiet and they're both staring at each other as though they're trying to figure something out.

Then Dexter says, "Hello, Hayden. Good to see you again."

My head whips over to look at Dexter, "Again?" I ask sharply, "Wait. You know each other?"

Hayden looks at me, then over to Dexter. His eyes squint, looking back and forth, seeming confused. He cocks his head to one side and slowly raises a finger pointing at Dexter, mouth slightly open, clearly not able to say a word.

"Dexter from the gallery, right?" He asks him.

"Yep." Dexter answers with a smack of his lips.

"From the gallery the other day, right?" Hayden asks Dexter inquisitively.

"Um. yes. We met yesterday?" Dexter says in a snarky tone, eyebrows raised, nodding his head yes sarcastically.

"The *gallery*?" my head whips over to Dexter; my eyes are both shocked and *very* concerned.

I look over at Hayden, who is completely straight-faced.

"Hayden? What is going on?" I ask him.

"I don't know. I..." Then, he stops and quickly looks at Dexter then back at me. His finger points a couple times at me while he's thinking hard.

Then it hits him.

"Wait... Samantha? Samantha Jenkins." His eyebrows drawn together in a frown, "S.E Jenkins," saying out loud to himself then shoots a look back at me.

"You're S.E. Jenkins?" asking as though not convinced and like the thought is ridiculous, piecing together how he knows me. His face looks flushed to me.

He's either surprised, embarrassed, or caught.

Heat starts rising throughout my body; I can't breathe.

I need air.

I look at him without saying anything, stare, but no words can come out.

What is he talking about?

How does he know Dexter? How does he know about the gallery? About *me*?

I look at him and in that second realize he's the man who bought my painting that night at the gallery, the one who was so cocky and rude.

He is also the one who smelled so good it took me a whole day to shake off how it made me feel.

I quickly grab my jacket and phone and do the only thing I can do.

I walk out, leave, in a full panic with my two very different worlds colliding.

Chapter 14

"What just happened?" Hayden asked Dexter.

"Well, Dr. Bryant, I think you just met, for the second time, I might add, the person whose paintings you like," Dexter waved his hand in the air and sat down; couldn't have made this up if he had tried.

He loved a good plot twist, but not so close to home.

"I didn't realize you were Sam's mothers' doctor," Dexter looked right at Hayden, "Did *you*?" Dexter knew he sounded accusatory because it was; Dexter had always been protective of Sam.

Plus, he loved cat fights.

"No!" Hayden said quickly and too loud.

"Well, not until now," he dropped his head, "I'm an idiot."

He sat down next to Dexter and dropped his head in his hands, feeling defeated.

Hayden didn't realize any of this but looking back he remembered Samantha from that night.

They met, yes, but it was fast. She was rambling on in an annoying way, he remembered feeling that night. She looked so different that night at the gallery than how he saw her daily now. She always looked professional and not at all looking like she did at the gallery with her hair in a hat and her freckles showing.

He had forgotten all about that night.

She was cute but also like a whirlwind and a spitfire; he remembers her now, and all the versions of her he's met connect into the swirling energy that is Samantha Jenkins.

But all he could do was sit there with Dexter regretting so much in one instance.

He had no words. No defense for how he acted that night.

Dexter looked at him, thinking how sad and pitiful he looked was kind of adorable.

The guy didn't realize who Sam was and this was painful to watch. Hayden was most certainly affected by these shenanigans, thought Dexter. Interesting, he wondered.

He is more than Sam's mom's doctor to Sam; Dexter wondered if this is what Sam was going to tell him today. Might even explain why she has been acting so strangely the last few days.

He came in for breakfast this morning determined to find out why Sam was so perky.

Here lies the reason, he thought.

But Dexter needed to know more and if anyone were equipped to find answers, he was the man for the job.

"Well, Dr. Bryant. I know this; you're an idiot if you let her walk away," Dexter told him matter-of-factly.

Hayden looked up from his hands, slowly raised his head toward Dexter and said, "Oh no," with a shake of his head, "I have done enough damage. Right now, I must be with the Jenkins family as their doctor. Right now, I need to stay far away from Samantha as anything else other than a doctor, someone that is here to help her mother, her family."

And then with his heart in his throat he asked, "Do you think she'll be ok? I did not connect her to the gallery, Dexter. As God as my witness, I didn't. Had I known, I would never have taken her to Sully's for dinner. I would never have…"

Dexter *knew* it! Now, this was up his alley and he needed to know more.

Dexter jumped in, giving the impression that he knew, "Oh, right, yes Sully's. She mentioned that to me." Dexter was lying but needed to bait him, and intel was worth a little white lie.

Hayden seemed surprised, "She did? Yeah, it was nice; nice to sit and talk to someone," Hayden said, "Without expectations and have it feel normal. Just simple. I haven't had normalcy since accepting this position as Dr. Piper's replacement. It really was supposed to be a night of talking and hanging out, but she was easy to talk to. Something about her…."

He stopped swallowing his words down and back into his heart. He was sharing too much. He needed to get back to work.

Dexter could see something was there and this guy was a sight for sore eyes; Sam needed to make some decisions.

But he knew Sam; she jumped into conflict head-on in the courtroom; it wasn't like her to run.

Something was there.

"Well, Sam is a tough turd," Dexter smiled and continued, "She can be tough, but she softens easily. She shares that piece of herself very little with very few," he stopped and thought for a hot second then said, "Ok. So, maybe it's just me. Case in point; S.E. Jenkins. Understand that she is not only one of my best friends and one hell of an attorney and she is awesome in every way, but she is private, Hayden. Very private. She comes from a family of love, but you have met her mother, some things just cannot be shared or discussed in that family. And right now, it's best we let her process this."

Dexter placed his hand on Hayden's arm, "Look, you seem like a good guy. Be patient. Right now, a *lot* is going on," he winked at Hayden, smiled, and said, "But if you want me to be Team Hayden, you better not break her heart."

"Whoa, Dexter, slow down," Hayden said, "we only went out for drinks and dinner. *Nothing* happened. Dexter, she just seems like someone I want to get to know," he shook his head to shake off his feelings, "Honestly, it was a bad idea."

Poor guy; Dexter could see he was a good man and he found himself feeling bad for them both because he could see Sam crushing on him. For Pete's sake, he almost was, too.

Who would have thought? Samantha, breaking hearts without dating anyone.

Dexter needed to talk to Samantha, but he would let her process this; she needed to feel it through.

If she needed him, he would be her first phone call; but until then this one needed to play out on its own without interference.

But, damn, Dexter thought to himself.

Dr. Hayden was adorable with his brownish-black hair that curled near his forehead like an Italian model and that jawline wasn't bad, either, Dexter thought to himself.

This made him sweat a little and he was nice to look at but not like his boyfriend, Rich, though; Dexter knew his man was the one.

"Well, I have to get back to the floor," Hayden told Dexter and stood up, "Thank you for listening and maybe I'll see you around," He turned to leave.

"Wait," Dexter said loudly and stood too, "What kind of cologne are you wearing?"

Hayden shook his head with a smile and answered, "It's deodorant," and headed to the floor to meet with the Jenkins'.

*　　　　　*　　　　　*　　　　　*　　　　　*

　　　*　　　　　*　　　　　*　　　　　*

I cannot get out to the courtyard fast enough.

I'm sweating like crazy although I feel my panic attack subsiding; I'm going to sit here and breathe in the air for as long as I can.

What the hell just happened.

How could he betray me?

He knew exactly who I was, who I am, and let me look like an idiot.

There you have it, folks; this is why I am alone, because of jerks out there that are dishonest and have no conscience.

I wasn't prepared to feel this way.

I enjoyed our night together, but these feelings are blasting through me. I wasn't prepared to have feelings for him this deep, not when he's done *nothing* to indicate that he's interested in me. He was a gentleman and there was something comfortable about him that night. It had me feeling something and wanting more for myself, even with my own mother.

I do remember him now, at the gallery; the more I think of that evening, the more I feel I have no clue who Hayden is.

I remember how he made me feel foolish at the gallery that night, left me feeling like a rambling moron.

How can this guy be that gentleman who shared his life with me? That man who made me feel good in my own skin, made me want to be more, do more, and feel more.

Is this the same man?

And how could I not remember?

If my head wasn't up my own ass, I would have put two and two together because something had been gnawing at me and I ignored it.

But he knows now; he knows me as an artist, as an attorney.

He frigging knows me as a patient's daughter.

This man knows way too much.

I feel exposed, vulnerable, and deep down I feel ridiculous, like he broke up with me.

He has done *nothing* to overstep any boundaries, giving me no indication that we are more than friends.

But what he *has* done has made me want more.

"One night Samantha. Hell, maybe all of three hours with the guy and you're behaving like an absurd schoolgirl." I say to myself.

I need to pull myself together and get up to Mom's room; I've been feeling sorry for myself for about an hour, and I know dad spent the night with her and I need to be with them.

But right now, I need space, so I get up from the bench and just walk; I walk right off the Mt. Sinai Hospital campus with the wind hitting my face.

I walk down E. 98th Street toward Park Ave.

I can't feel my body from the neck down, I'm numb with confusion. I'm confused about who Hayden is but even more confused about who I was and who I was becoming.

This whole thing was silly. What was I thinking? He knew who I was? And yet he still invited me out and didn't bring it up? What else is he hiding?

Hayden shared so much of his life, so much of his heart. I remember his face when he was speaking about the children he works with at the park, the fire in his eyes that showed how much it matters.

His burning desire to help them was contagious.

He was kind and friendly, but he didn't ask for my number.

What made me think there was more between us?

Maybe our banter and the way he teased me, but it was exhilarating.

The way the man that worked at the bar knew him and how Hayden seemed like a good guy even with people who were serving his food and drinks.

Maybe it was the way- I shake my head. This is stupid. He knew who I was, and he didn't share this with me. He knew a part of my life that I didn't want him to know about, it wasn't who I wanted him to know me to be.

It's safe to be Samantha Jenkins, successful, kind, straightforward, and confident. It was a side that always succeeded, and I wanted him to like me, so this side is best.

My mind is all over the place.

New York City is starting to spill out on the sidewalks for lunch and there are people everywhere.

Normally, I would park my butt on a bench and enjoy watching people but today I'm preoccupied thinking and walking because it feels much better than sitting down and feeling.

I cross over to Levington Ave and E. 86th Street; I feel my cheeks getting numb and my hands, although stuffed in my pockets, are cold. The wind between the buildings is brutal and I decide to stop and grab a coffee to warm up.

I've traveled a million times down this street and know the diner on E. 85th Street was there and open. I walk towards the diner, cross the street and hurry to the door. I opened the door, and the little rusty bell, like it had so many times since she and her father had been going since she was a kid, chimes, letting everyone know someone new just came in.

Mr. Jalbert looks up from the cash register as I sit at the small countertop that only has about eight bar stools.

"Hey kiddo!" Mr. Jalbert smiles.

He was almost like family, although I've only seen him here at the diner, he's known me since I was little and recognizes me right away.

Hearing him call me kiddo makes me feel tender and I swallow hard.

"Hello," I say quietly; I'm cold and exhausted.

"Sammy girl. What can I get you? How about a hot cocoa?" he suggests, smiling.

"Yes, please." I feel oddly meek and defeated.

I need a breather.

I watch him go over to the coffee pot area and grab a mug and while making me a hot cocoa, I watch his body and his hands move about behind the counter.

He's aged so much. He has short legs and a little belly that hangs over his belt line; he always wears the same blue shirt, has his apron on. When I was little I noticed he had an anchor tattoo on his lower arm. I asked him why and he told me he was Popeye and made a face and sang a song to me about living in a garbage can and eating spinach. I would always ask him to make "the face" each time I went in.

I asked my dad about the tattoo, and he shared that Mr. Jalbert was in the Navy and served in the Vietnam War. Now, looking back, I understand much more about Mr. Jalbert and how deep his loneliness must be as a veteran.

"Here you go. Served up just how you like!" He places my mug down and just like that, he brings a smile to my face because he served me my usual hot cocoa with whipped cream and shavings of chocolate sprinkled on top.

"Thank you, Mr. Jalbert," I say. He smiles, winks and the bell rings and he goes over to welcome his next guest to take their order.

I pull out my phone and place my mind on something else; I rest my head on one arm, drink my hot cocoa and browse through social media to escape.

"You know when your parents used to come in as teenagers in college they sat right over there in that booth. I'll never forget your parents back then. They were all of, maybe, 20 years old." Mr. Jalbert says, startling me.

"Seems like centuries ago. That's when my missus was around. She used to get up early in the morning with me, open the diner, and all the kids from college would come over for breakfast before their classes. Your folks, though, there was something different with them. Your mother was a firecracker. She would breeze through the door, giggling, smiling, laughing hysterically being chased by your old man and diving right into that booth over there and your father would follow right behind her, taking every opportunity to sit right next to her. Me and the missus knew they were in love." Mr. Jalbert shares while looking over to the booth, as though watching this memory in real time.

"Those were the days. When being in love was easy and everybody was excited to do just about anything. It was around 1977, the war had wrapped itself up and our welcoming committee of Americans were finally over us fighting the war. I couldn't go back to where I grew up. Everyone knew me and knew I was in the war, and nobody accepted me. So, I started life over here with this diner. And life was getting right back to normal. Watching kids like your parents, in love, is what got me and the missus through a lot of hard times here at the diner. Many times, we would join your parents when it got slow, sit down, and have coffee with them. They were in another world. But your mother...." he pauses, "was always full of life, always asking questions about us. Asking us questions about our families, asking me questions about being in the war, she always wanted to know more. They were something else."

I sit and listen and imagine; I've never heard stories like this before and it feels good. It brings me closer to them, it makes me want to know more.

"Mr. Jalbert. What was she like? My Mother? Back then?" I ask.

"Well, like I said, she was a spark plug. So sweet. Always dressed up nicely in her dresses. We knew she was probably from money, but never once could you tell by the way she treated others. Yep. She was all heart. Paying for others across the room, without them knowing if they looked like they could barely afford the price of milk. She had a heart of gold. Your grandfather, however," And Mr. Jalbert's lips turn at the corners, and he scowls, shakes his head left to right, "That man broke her."

My heart sinks; this is the first time I've heard anything about my parents as kids.

Broke her? I need to know more.

"Why? What happened?" I quickly ask.

"Nope, I've already said too much. Your parents are some good people, and I will always be grateful for their kindness."

"Mr. Jalbert!" I plead; I'm desperate to know, "Please share with me what happened. Mother is in the hospital, and I am losing my mind. So much has happened. I have no idea what to do, how to help but what I do know is I go home every night alone. I stay with my mother every day, alone and I'm sitting here, alone. I have no sisters or brothers. I have no one and I am not sure why." I am rambling, blubbering with tears rolling down my cheeks.

I know I look ridiculous with Mr. Jalbert on the other side of the counter, me sitting up on the stool, I am vulnerable, I feel naked, and I need to know more about her.

I need to know more about myself.

"Just one moment, Sammy," he says and walks over to his line cook and mumbles something who then looks over at me over Mr.

Jalbert's shoulder and smiles and nods, then turns back to his cook.

It looks like he's asking the line cook to help his customers for a moment while he speaks with me.

Mr. Jalbert then comes around the counter and pulls a stool right next to me, both of us facing the kitchen.

"Samantha," he says, and he places his hand over mine, "your dad. He loved your mama. He loved her like no other. But your grandfather had bigger plans for her. He finally caught up with her and where they hung out and I will never forget that day. My wife used to say that was the day that broke her. But your dad, he hung on for dear life. He wasn't about to let her go."

I can't keep my eyes off Mr. Jalbert. What is he talking about? Letting her go? My grandfather breaking her?

"Sammy, your grandpa, well, let's say they had money and with money back then came beliefs. Your mama, she had a spirit like no other. She was easy to talk to and would get fired up to defend the less than fortunate like no other. She would come in and have the best penmanship and take the chalk and write out specials up on the board, making it look real nice for my misses. Our hands were shaky so she would jump right up on the bar stools and make the board look like Times Square," He smiles, then he breathes in and slowly exhales.

"One of those days, when all the students were at school, your parents weren't; they played hooky that day. They came in, sat in the booth, sharing a piece of pie. Your grandpa received a call from the college; he learned a lot that day from that very phone call about where your mother was. He was about to learn a lot about what he didn't know about your mother. You see, your grandpa was on the board, and they called looking for his daughter who wasn't at school that day. Of course, his first stop was here, at the diner. This was the place where the local students hung out. He came barreling through that door," and Mr. Jalbert nods to the front door and continues, "I'm not sure his feet even hit the ground. Stomped himself right over to where your parents sat," and waved his hand towards a booth in the corner, "And took hold of his daughter by the back of the neck and started yelling at her." Mr. Jalbert paused, lost in memory.

"Yelling?" I'm on the edge of my seat.

Grabbing my mother? I never really knew my grandfather beyond Christmas' and holidays and birthdays; I only remember he was a very quiet man.

"What was he saying, Mr. Jalbert?" I beg to know more.

"I didn't get the full scoop. The missus and I could only hear bits and pieces but something about your mothers' studies. Guess she had switched her studies over to another subject. He enrolled her as a bookkeeper. Back in the 70's it was common to have women's next career step be in bookkeeping. Your grandpa had other plans for her and needed her to learn the books at his office and had sent her to school just for that. Sounded like she didn't have a choice about what she was going to be doing for work. And I guess your mother disobeyed his orders. Anyway, he looked over at your father and blamed "the boy" he called him. I remember my wife telling me that he was a father that didn't know his own daughter very well."

He paused again, shaking his head, "We didn't see your mama for weeks. Your father would come here all by himself. He was a lonely fella, your father. My wife would bring him food and he would barely eat. He would bring a book and bury himself in it, reading. That boy was a lost dog without his girl."

"But what about mother? Did they break up?" I asked.

"Well, you would think they had, but a couple of weeks later, they were back to being a couple. Your mother switched her studies back to bookkeeping and made a deal with your grandpa. She would study what he wanted, and she could be with your dad. That's what she had shared but I wasn't too convinced he knew your dad was back in the picture. We think she may have disobeyed another order from her old man."

My mouth dropped; I couldn't believe it! I had to ask, "What did she want to be?"

"You know, we never knew but I can tell you this; Ellie was never the same after. She was low key. Quiet. Kept to herself most of the time. When she was with your dad, she was always right beside him, holding right onto his arm. Almost like she was afraid to lose him again."

Mr. Jalbert shook his head, "Yep, those two became like kids to us. And your mother, she never stopped caring for us and never stopped paying for those who couldn't afford what she could."

He pauses, "That part, you probably know."

"Yes."

I knew because I had been delivering those envelopes for her for years.

"Yes, I know." I murmur again.

My heart aches for my mother; it's hard to picture how he described but I manage.

"Sammy, you've got yourself some good folks. They've been in love since they met. They always stuck together. You don't see that kind of love anymore. Nope. The kids now. They come in courting different girls and boys, every day. And you know what? Not one boy holds the door for a girl. Yup. Opens the door for themselves, but not for their date. These kids have a lot to learn from us folks but instead call us old fashioned. Too proud to listen is what they are." Mr. Jalbert rambles as he slowly walks away to start a fresh pot of coffee.

All I can think about is my parents, the way they were back then. It makes me smile.

The way she chose my father makes me smile even bigger.

But that sparkplug she was, where was it? Why hadn't I seen this side of her?

Where did she bury it?

I pull a $20 dollar bill out of my wallet and place it under my mug, then put on my jacket and start to walk out.

I want to be with my parents, I want to be a family with them.

Here I am sulking in my own stew and my mother is in a hospital with stage 3 pancreatic cancer; I need to suck it up and be there for them.

They were strong and I need to show them I am too.

"Hey where are you going, kid!?" He turns around and notices me heading to the door and I pause and turn around.

"Oh, I'm so sorry" and I rush over to Mr. Jalbert behind the counter and hug him; I can tell he is slightly uncomfortable, but he chuckles at me.

'No worries. Hey, send your folks my love."

"You bet I will," I say and head to the door, "Oh, Mr. Jalbert? *Thank you*." I tell him.

He smiles back and winks.

"You take care of yourself. And whatever it is that's ailing you? Nothing is so broken it can't be fixed."

Chapter 15

When I get to the hospital, Dr. Bryant is sitting with my parents in the chair, while my parents sit on the bed holding tight to one another.

Mom's face is white as a ghost and dad's eyes are red from crying.

My eyes dart at Hayden, and he looks away, "*Hayden*! What the hell is going on? Is this a conversation that I should be a part of?"

My father interjects, "Sammy. Sit down. Dr. Hayden was telling us your mother's results of her most recent CT scan."

"*Without me*? *Really* Hayden? Is this where we're at?" I ask pointing at me then to him.

Hayden is speechless but mother speaks up firmly but gently with, "Samantha Elizabeth. Sit down."

I continue to stand, and she looks at me.

"Please, honey," Mom pleads. She's different, weaker, something, but this time I need to listen.

I sit in the chair next to Hayden, but before I do I drag it about ten inches away from him, making it very clear we are not on the same side anymore.

"Samantha. I noticed in the last thirty or so hours that your mother's color was turning yellowish, so we tested her bilirubin levels and ordered another CT scan. Your mother has some biliary drainage into her pancreas; we're very concerned about setting her up with chemotherapy. In fact, drainage prevents us from continuing into the next phase of our treatment plan. We would like to do secondary surgery and approach treatment with a transpapillary stent. We do this with expandable metal stents."

Hayden takes a minute and a breath while giving me time to ask questions; I don't say a word.

"Your mother has agreed to this surgery but on her own terms."

I dart my eyes over to my mother and ask with my eyes what this means.

"Samantha, I would like to recover at home."

"Oh, hell no," I bypass my mother and turn to Hayden, "No. She is too far from the hospital, and I cannot be there as easily as I am now. No. Dad? You agree with this??"

My father says, "Sam. Let your mother make her own mind up. This is her body, and this is our home. Dr. Bryant has provided us with a solution that your mother feels could work."

My eyes race over to Hayden's, making eye contact that is clear I'm not happy right now.

His eyes are softer, telling me he has this.

"No," I tell him and make it personal I beg, "Hayden, please. She needs to stay here."

Hayden puts his hand on my knee for comfort and I immediately stiffen up and pull away.

"Samantha, I will be going to your parents' home every other day, if not daily. I will make any type of house call, at any time of the day. I will make it my personal responsibility to be her on-call doctor." His eyes meet my mother's, "I assure you, Eleanor. I will support you in anything you choose for your health if you agree that when I think it's time to come back to the hospital, you will be on board."

Mother's face has a warm smile. She closes her eyes for a second and opens them and looks at Dr. Bryant, "I promise. I promise. Doctor's orders." Mom grabs dad's hand and raises her other, beckoning me to come to her.

I get up and hold her hand. If our time together, yesterday, hadn't happened, I would not have recognized this woman.

'Doctor, we are a team, and you just became part of us. Thank you. Thank you so much." she says to Hayden.

Every inch of me is screaming, "No. No we are *not a team with him,*" inside.

She has no idea what she just arranged, and he has no idea what he just agreed to.

 Who is this woman?

The gardener wasn't even allowed in the house to use the bathroom, let alone her doctor.

I feel my mind racing like a five-lane freeway, going in every direction.

I look at both my parents and their calm in Hayden's presence; this is not only surreal but staggering. I am at odds with myself, with the three of them, and every corner of my mind is against this decision.

"Mother," I stand and turn to my parents, "I am going to get some air and a cup of coffee. Can I get you anything?"

Dad understands I need time and says, "Sure, Sammy that would be wonderful," and stands and kisses my cheek.

I can't get out of this room fast enough.

I high tail it to the hallway and see the sign for the stairs and decided to take them to the cafeteria.

I need to blow off some steam.

I swing the door open and start racing down the stairs as fast as I can, my heart pumping and I pause on the second floor, leaning my whole body on the railing, trying to catch my breath.

I hear my name, "Samantha! Wait up!"

I look up the stairwell and see its Hayden.

"Hayden, just go," I turn and continue down to the first floor.

But he doesn't stop.

I hear his shoes barreling down the stairs as fast as he can move, "Sam, no. Please, we need to talk."

"Haven't you done enough, Hayden? Just go do your job and be a doctor and I will do mine and be a daughter," I say sharply.

He catches up to me and on my heels when he stops and says softly, "Sam. Please?"

He catches me off guard and his voice stops me in my tracks; I turn to him not knowing how close he truly is and we end up nearly nose to nose.

"Sam, I didn't know who you were, I didn't recognize you. I promise you, Samantha, that's the truth."

I hear in his voice that he's being honest, but my truth is this, "Hayden, it doesn't matter. It is what it is" I say and turn to walk away.

"It is what it is?" he questions sarcastically.

He stands there looking after me as I walk away.

He is *killing* me. I need to walk away but everything about his voice, his eyes, make me want to say things, make me want him to keep chasing after me.

I whip my body around to him, a whole staircase between us, which is far more comfortable.

"Hayden. Please, just stop. Ok, so, fine. Yes, you know who I am.... You know what I do…You know my parents and are now in charge of my mother's health. Can you just focus on her for now? Honestly, I am exhausted. But do us all a favor. Please don't do *any more* damage and tell my parents about me and my art. Clearly, Hayden they don't know and you…. Well… now, you *do*. Just keep that to yourself, help my mother, and stay as far away from me as you can."

He takes a step down, then stops.

"You mean that, Samantha?" he asks me with a hurt in his eyes that stings me.

"I… no… I. Hayden," I don't know what to say; this man touches a part of me that I have never known existed before the last few days.

He interrupts me.

"Samantha, look, I am trying here. I'm trying to do two jobs here. I am trying to help your parents and most importantly your mother in her recovery but, Samantha Jenkins, there is something about their daughter that I'm trying to understand and ignore. You're not the only one who feels pulled in two different directions."

This takes me by surprise, and I think everything about my body language and face shows how taken aback I am.

I say to him in an almost whisper, "Hayden, we had one dinner together."

He walks down the steps to me, "Really? Because I am confident it was more than that. When I look back at the night at the gallery there was something about you, something fiery and passionate that I can't shake. Ever since that night and after meeting you, Samantha, every time I'm around you, I feel like we've known each other before. Since then, every time I get ready to come to the hospital, I wonder if I'll see you, I hope that I will. Look, I don't know what's going on except that it matters to me that you're so upset. It matters to me that you feel betrayed, and it matters to me that your mom needs my help. For now, let's help your mom, but I need to know we, you, and me, are ok."

I can't breathe.

This boy, this man, is beautiful.

He sounds beautiful, he smells beautiful, and the puppy dog eyes staring into my soul are beautiful.

Before I can think I answer, "Hayden..." and step toward him.

I feel him reach for my hand and the lump in my throat as my chin begins to quiver; I feel the tears well up.

I feel weak and raw, vulnerable, and helpless as I say, "Help my mother. She's all I have. Please, Hayden, don't let her die."

Chapter 16

Walking home from school every day is awesome now that I'm twelve years old.

Mother finally trusts me after a couple of practice runs and now walking home feels so good with my Mp3 player and my headset playing Hillary Duff songs.

I love walking home; I wave to my neighbors while listening to music and hopscotch to pretend squares along the way.

I feel like I'm sixteen years old. Older, even. I reach into my pocket looking for a stick of gum only to feel my lucky coin.

When I was little, mother and I went to the market and there was this little Asian lady selling coins with trees engraved on them. Mother bought me one and she knelt to me and said, "Keep this with you, Samantha Elizabeth. When you feel afraid or need strength, reach into your pocket, and feel this coin and let it remind you to never forget where you came from. We are women of strength and courage; never forget that."

That coin has been in my pocket every day of school since kindergarten because every morning mother says, "Do we have our lucky coin?"

I'm playing with it as I turn the corner near the gates of the house and see mother at the door looking toward me, waving me in almost frantically.

My heart starts racing.

She looks like she's been crying, her face is red as she waves for me to hurry; I pull out my earphones and place them in my back pocket, book it to the house.

"Mom, are you okay?" I say with my hands on my waist holding onto my stitch in my side, breathing heavily from running.

"Samantha, I need you to get in this house. I just learned Lucille is coming over for a visit and Ms. Winn didn't come by to clean and I cannot make this house shine by myself," Mother says desperately, "Please, let's put some fire under those feet. I need help cleaning right now!"

I know when I hear this, this house needs to be cleaned; mother never lets anyone in our home with even one speck of dust sitting on the shelf and trust me, mom's friend, Lucille will find the dust, no matter where it is.

"Oh shit!" I murmur under my breath, and I take off into the house ready to clean.

"*WHAT DID YOU SAY YOUNG LADY?*" Mother demands and I stop and stiffen.

I slowly look over at her to read her face, see whether she heard me and wants me to repeat it or if she knows what I said and is just forcing me to repeat it.

I say, "Let's not quit, mother," and jump right in ready to clean our house from top to bottom.

"Hello? Sam? Sam? The door was unlocked, so I walked in. Are you here?" Dexter is yelling from the bottom of the staircase in a high-pitched voice, "Hello?"

It jumps me right out of my memories of cleaning as a child with my mom.

I look up and Dexter is approaching me as I wash each spindle of my parents' staircase on all fours.

"Lord, girl what are you doing?" Dexter is obviously appalled at my appearance.

I know I look terrible with filth all over my clothes, my face exhausted from cleaning, not to mention, I haven't bothered combing my hair.

I sit back on my legs, throw my rag in the mop bucket, and say, "I know I look like shit, Dex, but mom got out of surgery yesterday and I had twenty-four hours to make this place clean. Dexter, Hayden is coming over and Mom hates it when this place is a hot mess. It needs to be cleaned," I barely got those words out.

I am ex*hausted*; I feel beaten up. The last three days are like a blur, and it all feels like a dream.

"If I thought things were put on hold in my life before this with her being sick, they really are now. Look, I feel defeated."

And I do. I have deadlines at work, dad's fridge has mold growing out of leftovers from three weeks ago, my painting for the fundraiser needs to be completed, and, at this point, my cat doesn't even recognize me when I go home at night.

Not to mention, Dr Bryant is mom's on call Doctor and seeing him is a pain in my ass and a butterfly in my gut.

"I know sweetie," He walks up the stairs to me and pulls me to stand, looks at me, cups his hand on my chin and says, "Damn girl, did you brush today?"

He grimaces and I burst out laughing.

"Shut it," I say and walk past him down the stairs as he follows me.

"I have barely changed my underwear, Dexter, so back off. This place has to be cleaned, disinfected, and I am the only one who can do this the way mother likes before she comes home."

"Yeah, yeah, yeah, "Dexter says sarcastically, and looks around then says with a smile, "No offense sweetheart, but you're no Martha Stewart, so how about I help you."

Without letting me answer, he grabs the plastic gloves out of my hand, snaps them making a popping noise, looks back, and winks at me.

He grabs the Windex and Lysol out of the cleaners cart I'm using, raising the Lysol above his head and starts to spray a path to the kitchen where he immediately begins to wash the windows.

I join Dexter in the kitchen and begin cleaning the countertop and all the handles of the cabinets.

"So, tell me, any news of how the surgery went?" Dexter asks as we clean steadily, in sync with one another.

"Yeah, Dr. Piper and Hayden told us yesterday that her levels are good, her body is just tired, " he says. Trying to heal and recover. She came out of it a little groggy and is getting a cold, I guess, but hell-bent on coming home. I was hoping she'd changed her mind, but she seems more determined than ever to be home." I tell Dexter as I am scrubbing madly around the sink sweating like the chubby girl I was in 1st grade gym class.

"She is a tough turd, that woman, not to be mean, but she is way too stubborn to die, Sammy. No offense, but God doesn't want that girl yet, he would get nothing done up there. She would be competing to be in charge."

This makes me smile.

"I know you're not wrong. That woman, she... she does everything so good, so big. Never missing a beat. I think when I was little, I decided right away, I could never be the woman she is, she just does everything so well. My mother is like the mansions down the road in the cul-de-sac. Airtight, perfect, so clean. But,

Dexter, me? I'm more of a fixer upper on the outskirts of Jersey," I say and burst out laughing.

Dexter looks over at me, raises an eyebrow and says, "Well, I like fixer uppers because they have good bones and are rare. Besides, you tell me that every fixer upper show on TLC has a uniqueness about them that no other modern-day house has. Shit girl, I love my fixer upper. Jenkins, you are far better than you give yourself credit for. Plus, I think Hayden likes fixer uppers, too."

The sound of his name makes my heartbeat harder; he makes my whole-body smile just wanting to see him.

"Dexter, you should have seen him with mother yesterday."

I pause in thought then continue, "He was so good. She even reached up and gave him a little face pat and told him he was like her husband, a "rare find". If this woman could, she would take him home."

"Um, Sam?" Dexter says and I look over at him.

"She *is* taking him home," he says and smirks.

"Yup," I smack my lips together, making a noise, "She sure is".

We clean the house from top to bottom for the rest of the afternoon to 90's music and together we make it sparkle and jamming with old songs, we dance for hours.

Dexter grabs the remote and pretends it's a microphone, lip-syncing to Ace of Base's *The Sign*.

We laugh and clean and clean and laugh and it's exactly what I need, and Dexter can deliver an escape while getting stuff done.

"What a day!" Dexter says and collapses on the white velvet couch then kicks his feet up over the arm.

"No kidding! I could not have done it without you, though, seriously, I could *not* have."

"Shit, we are a team Jenkins, in and out of work." He blows a kiss to where I'm sitting in dad's recliner.

I get up and pour a glass of wine for us both from the bar near the fireplace.

"Tell me Dex," I say as I pass him his glass, "Do you think Hayden really knew me from the gallery?"

"No, Sam, I do not," He says matter-of-factly, "And honestly I am glad he knows now. I'm glad for you! Sammy, I didn't come out to my parents for well over ten years because I was afraid they would never accept me. I had this part of me that I couldn't share, and it became a secret and my secret turned into my shame. Shame is a slow and silent killer. I had nothing to be ashamed of and you don't, either. I don't want you to feel this way over something you love so well."

"Dexter, I love you, and I love who you are," He makes my heart happy. He is my dear best friend and sometimes I forget that he, too, has his own history that he endured.

I want to be half the friend for him that he is for me.

'Shit girl don't get all sentimental on me. This boy, Hayden? He likes you, Sammy. He likes you from the hospital with your mama and now that he knows you from the night at the gallery, I know he likes you even more. You should have seen him at breakfast when you walked away. I can tell he cares for you. You got up and left and I could see in his eyes that half of him had left with you. He cares. This guy is a good one, Sam. Even your mom is crushing on him," he pokes fun at me, and we laugh.

He's right.

This one *is* a good catch. I knew it when I met him, and I know it now. I just need to figure it all out. This is beyond what I'm good at, beyond what I expected. But for now, I need to be present for mom and dad.

It's just this man that has my mind spinning.

"We are *home*, Sam. Can you give me a hand helping mom into the house?"

"Shit!" I look over at Dexter and we jump up and go to the entryway where dad is standing with bags all along his arms and a flowerpot in his hand.

"Dad. Here, let me take these!" I unload him and load Dexter up with the items to take in the kitchen. Dexter carries all the belongings into the kitchen, as I step out onto the front stoop where Mom is in the passenger seat trying to get out.

I hear dad go toward the car giving her hell as she tries to get out by herself, "No, honey we are coming," I scurry over to the car and place her arm around my neck to help her out.

My mother whispers in my ear, "He thinks he is in charge, but he is *not.*"

I smile without her seeing; she is a mighty woman who is about to have the time of her life fighting off people trying to help her.

"Dr. Bryant will be here in two hours, the house is a mess. Sam, can you help me clean it up?" she asks.

"Mom, it's clean. Dexter and I took care of it." I reassure her.

"Oh, that Dexter. He is a gem. A good cleaner, though?" She looks at me concerned.

"Yes, mom! Don't worry. It's clean!" I say to her hoping Dexter isn't hearing this.

This woman is impossible.

Two hours? Here? Already? Hayden is coming *here*?

We walk mother into the house and bring her into the living room and lay her on the couch to rest; I place the blanket over her lap.

I hurriedly go into the kitchen and straight over to Dexter.

"Dexter! He is coming here in *two hours*. I look like shit. I need to jump in the shower and do something with this," and I wave my hand around my head then down my body to indicate everything.

"Well get your ass in that shower. I have to run home for Rich, we have plans tonight and I have to get ready. Love you, kid," He kisses my cheek, grabs his keys, and heads to the door.

"Hey Dexter. Thank you!" He turns to me in the doorway and peeks back in, then winks, "I got your back girl."

I walk back into the living room where dad is sitting at the head of the couch with mother's head in his lap. She lay, content, his hand gently running over her hair. She already has her eyes closed.

I pass them quietly to head upstairs and mother says with her eyes shut, as though she can see me, going upstairs, "I hope you're taking a shower, Samantha. You look like you were caught in a hurricane. My doctor will be here soon."

"Yes, mother," I yell down the stairs and head immediately to the shower.

A shower after a day of cleaning feels so good.

My body aches so badly.

I haven't cleaned like this in years, I have such a small apartment that I never need a cleaner. It's just me and my cat and living simply is what we do. The only mess is my painting area but that's off limits and I know where everything is; my paints, brushes.

It looks a mess, but to me it was perfect.

I feel the hot water running over my head and let the power of it hit the top of my back; perfection. I shampoo my hair, because I only do so every three days for fear of it drying out.

My mother told me all the oils in my hair are needed to moisturize it naturally and never to wash it every day.

My mind moves to Hayden's hair, how dark his hair is and how the ends curl up, almost wispy. Not short and not too long. He has such beautiful hair; I wonder what it smells like.

What I wouldn't give to run my fingers through his hair or hell, even smell his hair, just once. It was almost as beautiful as his hands. I noticed his hands immediately when I met him. He reached out to shake my hand and I noticed how soft they were. You can tell he took care of them. They were almost pretty boy hands.

Just the thought of this man hiking, sweating, while I felt the heat of the water hit my body pulls my mind in a direction I need to avoid going in.

I quickly switch over to the cold water and for a second let the cold sting my body, let my pores close up and turn the water off, reach for a towel and wrap my body up with a second towel for my hair.

And there I stand in front of my mirror.

This is what I do; I stare at myself and wonder where on earth my person is.

Would they like this body? Could they see past my hips, or my freckles? Oh man, what about this boring face? What about this plain Jane face would he like most.

I've never taken much interest in wearing makeup as hard as I have tried.

I have a decent, curvy body but never had an urge to decorate and design myself to be anything other than me, although I wear cute outfits that highlight my figure.

But today I suppose it wouldn't hurt to look decent, to look like the best version of me.

I open my closet to the clothes I left behind when I moved out; Mother has stored her things in my closet and half are her clothes and half are mine.

I sift through the clothes, moving past shirts, skirts, sweaters and find a cute navy-blue camisole that I slip over my head. I haven't seen this before. Perhaps it was an oldie of mine that I never wore. I reach in for a sweater that buttons up and I button it up to the second to last near my breast, showing the lace part of the cami.

I dig into the pants and my old jeans from twelfth grade catch my eye; these are cute. I put one leg in, then the other.

These used to be baggy and not as snug as they are now; I button them and turn to the mirror, glance at my butt, "Oh boy, these are a little fitted".

"Dear Lord, how does someone wear their jeans so tight?" I say out loud; these suckers are giving me a wedgie from hell, but they look cute on me. I stand in the mirror looking at myself.

"Not bad."

I unbutton the top of my sweater, then another, leaving only two buttons on the bottom. For a second, I feel good about how I look.

Attractive.

I go into the bathroom and blow-dry my hair upside down swinging my hair right side up looking fresh but a wee bit like Farrah Fawcett in the 80's.

I pull out my iron underneath the sink from when I used to crimp my hair and reattach the flat iron to the end.

I carefully iron each section until my hair falls past my shoulders looking nice and slick.

I smile and dab lip gloss on my lips. "This will do."

I start downstairs and hear a murmur of noise; sounds like we have company earlier than we expected. Perhaps Lucille and her husband are visiting.

I start down the stairs and towards the dining room where the voices are coming from.

Mother is sitting at the table with soup in front of her that looks like it was brought over.

"Honey! Look who brought me dinner!" Mother says as she sits all bundled up in a sweater and blanket keeping her warm.

I look over to Hayden as he comes around the corner from the kitchen with two mugs of tea in his hands and leans down to give mother hers.

"Hello, Samantha," he says, smiling at me although he avoids eye contact, "I stopped by Jimmy's and grabbed your mom some soup.

I didn't realize you were going to be here, or I would have brought you some, too."

My heart hits the floor and I am confident my mouth is hanging open; he looks so good. He wears faded jeans with running shoes, a flannel shirt, and a baseball cap.

This man is so gorgeous I can barely breathe.

"Hayden! Hi! You're early!" is all I can say.

"I'm sorry! Was I supposed to be here later?" He looks over at mother.

"No, don't worry one bit Hayden, you may as well pack a bag and stay! My home is your home!" she says to him, smiling big and looking from me to him. She glances at me and cocks her head slightly, raises one eyebrow because she can tell I'm fumbling and maybe gives the dirty eyeball because I sound rude.

"Oh Gosh no. *No.* I just didn't know you were here. Of course, you're welcome anytime." I need to get myself back on track, "Hayden, I would offer you a drink, but it looks like you and mother have it under control!"

"He sure does!" Dad says following right behind him, "Hayden, help yourself to anything you need. Maybe Sam can go out to the grocery store and grab some items," he looks over at me. "Your mother and I can make you a list."

"Sure. Yes. Yes. Sure, I can do that. Yeah." I respond tentatively.

But my mother has a different agenda and this time it's blatantly obvious when she says, "Hayden, maybe you can join Samantha and grab some groceries and feel free to grab yourself some snacks to keep here, for when you visit." She says to him, glances over at me, and smirks.

She knows exactly what she's doing- I look over at Hayden and he smiles at me in a way that suggests maybe he knows, too.

"Ok, I'll grab my jacket," I reach over to the table and grab the list she's handing to me then to the foyer for my coat. I open the front door to get some air and feel the cold winter wind caress my face that's sweating from the stuffiness of the house.

What the hell is going on right now?

It's like I have zero control over my life.

Mother is single-handedly running the show on her health while also playing matchmaker and whatever else is up her sleeve, all while fighting cancer. She is ruthless and I feel more vulnerable than ever.

Hayden clears his throat as he walks outside to me, and I look at him.

"Hayden, I am so sorry. She is absolutely bullheaded. I'm not sure what she's trying to do here but I ..." I start but Hayden interrupts and takes a step closer to me; I feel him put his warm hand in mine.

He faces me and says in almost a soft whisper, "Jenkins, I think we both know what she's doing."

The corners of his mouth turn up in a way that shows me he doesn't mind.

My body freezes still; he can tell I'm startled by his hand in mine.

He pulls away slightly, "I'm sorry. I didn't mean to."

"No," I say, and I slide my fingers back through his, "It's ok. I mean if it's ok with you?"

He smiles and brings my hand to his lips and kisses it and says, "It's ok. This is okay, too, I hope."

I let him take my hand and look at him, then at our entwined fingers between us.

I peer at him, and he smiles at me.

I whisper back, "More than okay, Dr. Bryant."

Chapter 17

My fingers run across the brush while I determine if my isolation coat is complete; I have less than six hours to seal this piece and get it to the fundraiser that starts at 3pm.

My fingers move from brush to brush, scanning each one, looking at how beautiful they are.

It's been two days since I've seen Hayden and I can't stop thinking about him; the way he touched my fingers, the way his lips pressed against my hand.

This man is beautiful, everything about him, even the way he is with Mother.

Even the way she is with him.

He makes me want to be better; he makes me want more.

For the last two days, he has been with my parents, and I used the time to get caught up at work. I've spent almost four weeks away from the office and my mind needed to be cleared not to mention Dexter's desk.

But Hayden hasn't stopped texting me updates about mother.

I grab my varnish spray, place it aside, and instead, grab my phone. I scroll to his texts and reread them. I've read them multiple times; am I reading too much into them? Is he just flirty? Each time I read them I second guess his intentions and second guess why he would want me.

Hey Sam. Your mom has caught a nasty cold. Probably from germs at the hospital, and the stress of the last couple of weeks, but I'm keeping an eye on her.

Thank you so much, Hayden. I cannot tell you how grateful I am that you're there. Dad told me they called you late last night again to come by. I'm so sorry. If at any time you think she should go back to the hospital, don't hesitate to tell her. PLEASE! And BTW how are you?

I know. I already mentioned it to your mom. Her lungs are what worries me. I see this a lot. Pneumonia with older people when they're going through things like this. I'll keep an eye out. She is set on staying home and I'm good with taking care of her there. I hope you're getting your work done. Hope to see you soon, though. Let's have coffee.

Yes. For sure. I would love that… call me if you need me. I mean with my mother. Call me if she needs me. Hitting the hay right now. Exhausted but getting so much done.

Night, Jenkins

Night, Dr. Bryant

*   *   *   *   *   **

Morning Beautiful! Hope you slept well.

Morning, Hayden. Having coffee right now and finishing up the painting. It's so beautiful outside. We had snow last night! I love the first snowfall, just not the ones that come after, lol. You get it, right?

I do. In New Hampshire, the first snowfall I would go sledding. Have you ever gone sledding before?

You do know whose daughter I am, right? No, I haven't, but it sounds fun.

Lol. Well, Ms. Jenkins, not only will I be teaching you how to ride a bike, but I will teach you how to sled. (I am keeping a list.)

Ok. I'm in. I just need to think of things I can teach you. For now, we will stick with "how to take care of my mother with a smile". How is she today?

I just got to your parents' house, and she sounds pretty rough. Her breathing is labored, almost wheezing. I listened to her lungs, and I have concerns about possible fluid buildup. I put her on antibiotics, but she is still refusing to go to the hospital. But I am here. Just come by when you have the chance. I know she would love to see you. Me too if I'm here.

Yes I can come by tonight. Ok. Call me if there is an emergency. Lord knows they won't! See you tonight!

*   *   *   *   *

Sorry I missed you tonight. Mom was sleeping the whole time when I came by. Her breathing sounded awful. Dad said I just missed you.

Hey, Jenkins. Yeah, I had an emergency at the hospital. I gave your mom some medicine to rest and knew she would be out for the night. You must have been out late because I left at 8pm.

Yes, court lasted until 4:30 then I went back to the office because I had another meeting at 5:30 with a new client that I had blew off too long and I had to get it done. I was hoping to see you. You may have forgotten who I am. Feels like I haven't seen you in a while.

You're telling me. I miss you, Jenkins.

I miss you, too.

Oh. Tomorrow I have to jet out around 2ish from your parents but will be back after dinner. Just letting you know in case you need me.

Ok! Hope everything is ok.

Oh Yeah everything is fine. Just have things to do at the hospital.

Sure! Ok. Hey, get rest too, Hayden. I know you're burning the candle at both ends.

Ok lol. The last time I heard that saying was back home. Are you sure you're not 65 years old?

Sometimes I think so. Today, not so much. Have a good night.

Night, Jenkins.

Night, Hayden.

 Reading his texts over makes me believe he is thinking of me as much as I am of him.

This man has me already; I just hope I'm not overthinking us.

I pull the varnish out. It's important I varnish my paintings or the lifespan of them will be no longer than 5 years.

I think of varnishing my painting a lot like a wedding cake; you have the fragile cake, and it needs the fondant icing to seal it, to protect it. That was a lot like varnishing to me. It protects my work.

I begin applying my varnishing with my wider brush, that way it doesn't leave brush strokes, but applies evenly.

Once I complete this step, I sit back and take a look at my painting.

This couple on their childhood swings, this older couple with their whole life behind them and their view now is of only each other.

I want to find the one I can grow old with, I want to watch my future husband's hands as the skin ages. I want to hold hands on a swing set with the man I marry. I get so lost in the fantasy of my paintings, but this painting means more than others. I mean, this could easily be my parents. They were so young when they met. They may have had their own place, like a swing set. Maybe their place was the booth at Mr. Jalbert's. That would be where they would always find one another and the love they first felt. I wonder if Hayden is to be mine, where will our place be?

I am not sure we would even have a place. We met at the gallery, then again at the hospital and I found no romance in either.

Maybe we will never have our beginning place.

With Hayden, that's ok. I feel like no matter where we are, my place will always be with him.

Am I moving too fast? Or are we moving too slow? I don't even know our timetable except that every single time he tells me a piece of him or what he wants to do, I want him to show me.

There is a mystery about Hayden that makes me want to know more.

A country boy doctor from New Hampshire who ended up in NYC.

How he grew up, his full story, I want to know it all. He knows so much about me, my life. He basically was inserted into our life and has to learn as he goes but I still know very little about him.

I look at my watch; it's time to head to the fundraiser.

I gently touch my painting and see it's good to go, but in case it's still a tad fragile, I cover it with parchment paper for travel and head out.

Chapter 18

I place myself, standing, at the back of the auditorium where I can see everyone attending the auction.

I see the stage has three 8 ft long tables *full* of donated items alongside plenty of others on easels, including mine.

The place is packed wall to wall and it's pretty amazing to see such a crowd, lots of people with white lab coats. I think they're on break from the hospital to make bids of their own.

I've been to plenty of auctions like this and it's always fun to watch.

This one has rows of people, and each row has a person assigned to see who in the row is bidding; I've been to some auctions where people would shout bid after bid, bidding over one another only to be more competitive, surpassing the value of the items, just to win.

It was fun; I hope this one brings in good money.

"Ms. Jenkins!!!" I hear someone yelling my name from the middle of the room.

I swing my head over toward the voice and see Charlene waving her hand, frantically trying to get my attention.

She cups her hand over her mouth and says, "Thank you!" and gives me a thumbs up.

She is so adorable, mom's nurse. She did keep my donation a secret, which I didn't see coming.

I wave back and return her thumbs up with one of my own.

The hospital staff has been so wonderful with my mother, we could not have asked for a better team. It's amazing watching how much heart they put into their jobs because I never realized before how thankless their jobs are. I hope with auctions like this, they feel gratitude from all of us for taking care of our loved ones while most likely being away from their own loved ones.

Medical staff definitely work hard, I've seen it firsthand now. I also see how quickly they become like family.

The lights lower in the auditorium but enough so we can still see amongst one another and the doors to the left open wide; about a dozen medical staff bring in children and adults in wheelchairs and park them right in the front row to watch.

What a visual of my why; this is why I donated the piece in the first place.

The head of the hospital comes on stage to the podium and introduces himself, then gives us a history of the auction for the oncology wing. He then goes into the many thanks to the nurses and the committee that put the whole auction together and those that donated. A round of applause cheers the room.

She shares that she especially wants to thank the head of the committee for her countless hours and great spirit in making sure today was a success and introduces Charlene.

"Charlene, could you please stand up so we can give you a great big thank you for your hard work?" the president says and Charlene pops right up from the crowd waving like a mayor in a parade, or a Miss America contestant.

I just love this girl, she is such a breath of fresh air! She waves for long that the president says, "Thank you, Charlene. Yes, thank you" and gives her a nod to sit down.

The auctioneer is introduced next, and the auction begins.

Back and forth, back, and forth, one item after another. Arms are flying in the air. The runners are raising their hands left and right. It's all so very well-orchestrated.

"Two hundred, two hundred fifty, three hundred, three hundred twenty dollars, going once going twice sold to row M seat?"

"25," the runner shouts back.

One item goes for a pretty long time bid after bid, it's dinner tickets to a Broadway show for two. The ladies are raising their hands so fast because this show has been sold out for some time. This was a great item to donate to the cause.

I see my item is coming up; I watch as the stage helpers prep it and carry it over to the auctioneer.

"Next, we have this wonderful 24x30 acrylic painting. Folks this is a beautiful painting that very resembles the work of Monet. In this specific piece, the focal point is a lovely, aged couple on a swing-set that appears to nurture the love they have for one another. Joined at the hands, while swinging this couple represents love, harmony and easily stimulates the desire and need to be loved. Let's start the bidding at $400."

My heart is beating so fast; I look around the room, hoping someone bids. My biggest fear is that the place will become quiet and stay that way.

"$450 row B, we have $500 Row T, $600, $600 in Row S anyone for $700?"

"$900!" we hear from the back.

"900 Row T, we have $975 back to Row B."

"We have $1050 in Row T, $1200 Row B $1400? Row T going once, $1400 Row T, wow, folks we have $1700 back to Row B."

I am on my tippy toes trying to see who is in Row T and it looks like it's an older woman in her 70's, frail but determined. I step a little closer hoping to catch who was in Row B but just can't get a look at who it is; whoever it is, they're relentless.

"Do we have $1800? Do we have $1775? Do we have $1750?"

The little lady in Row T sits back down and shakes her head no.

"Sold to Row B seat?" and the runner responds with Seat 14.

The crowd cheers.

I cannot believe my eyes or ears. My painting. This is incredible but without question brings me to tears. To give back to this community is the very least I can do. The past four weeks have been my hell, my family's hell, but we have learned very quickly that it takes a village even if the head chief, my mother, doesn't want help. This community has taught us about unconditional giving and unconditional helping and this painting was the least I could do.

The auction comes to an end, and I am about to leave, when Charlene comes running up to me and slings her arms around my neck before I know it was her.

I was in the middle of wiping away my tears when she grabbed hold of me.

"Oh, Charlene, hi" I say to her, surprised by the amount of affection she's laying on me, but I love it, I do. I love it because she's a good person.

"Oh Ms. Jenkins. Can you believe how much it went for! They are squaring away and paying. Let's go see who bought it!" She grabs my hand and is yanking me down the aisles to the front where the cashiers on site are collecting the money for the items.

I look around and see the patients in the chairs, smiling and chatting away with people, thanking everyone for coming. I draw closer to the cashier line when I bump right into someone and see Hayden.

"Hayden. Hey! I didn't know you were coming." I say.

"Samantha. Hey! It's so good so see you," he reached out to me and kisses me on the cheek.

Charlene is standing there and looks from me to him and says, "Okie dokie. Y'all have a wonderful" as she is feeling awkward and disappears.

"Excuse me, Dr. Bryant, that'll be $1800," the cashier says to Hayden and he reaches in his back pocket for his wallet and pulls out his credit card and hands it to the cashier.

I look at the cashier then at Hayden.

"Hayden?"

He turns back to me "Yeah?" and then continues to sign his name on the credit card slip.

"Wait. Hayden, did you buy that painting?" and I point to it towards the painting on the stage, my painting.

He turns back to me and says, "Yeah why? You like it?"

"Hayden," I feel my face turning red, "Hayden, I painted it."

He turns back at me and squints his eyes and places his hand on my arm with a panicked look in his eyes.

"Samantha I didn't know. I promise, I didn't know." He says.

I inhale and search his eyes for the truth only to find myself lost in them. I feel my heart soften and in this moment, this moment where I feel my heart gush onto the floor between us, leaving me feeling alive and vulnerable.

I want to share with him how much I think about him and care about him.

How beautiful his hair is, his hands are, how soft his lips feel on my cheek, on my hand. I want to tell him I want to spend every moment with him.

Instead, I gently take his hand from my arm, take his face in my hands, and kiss him.

I kiss him softly, then feel him kiss me back, can feel that he wants this as much as I do.

His lips are warm, his skin in my hands soft.

It's just me and Hayden on the whole planet right now.

"Doctor Bryant, your receipt."

He breaks our kiss, thanks the cashier, then looks at me and says, "Gosh, Jenkins, you are beautiful."

Chapter 19

I wake up at 3am to my cell phone ringing; it's my dad.

"Honey, you need to come home. Your mother is not well."

I don't get a chance to say hello because my phone receives a text from Hayden.

"You need to come to your parents. It's your mom. She isn't doing well."

I go back to my phone where dad is on the line.

"Dad. I'll be right there," I assure him.

"Ok. Honey, wait...Sammy?" He says as I go to end our call, but I hear him say my name just in time.

"Yeah, Daddy?"

"When you come, just hold her hand. Just be present." He says.

I feel my heart drop; his voice is desperate.

I say calmly, "Yes, Daddy. I will be there soon."

I end the call, my heart beating super-fast and throwing myself into gear.

I grab pants and put them on, throw a sweatshirt over my head, twisting my arms in every direction, trying to wake myself up, then throw my hair up in a bun.

"What in the world is happening? She got worse?" I think to myself.

I forget that Hayden sent me a text and grab my phone.

"Dad called. I will be there soon. On my way."

I slip my sneakers on, grab my bag, and stop in my tracks, look around.

What else do I need?

What am I forgetting? My eyes scour the room.

In a flash, I know. I run to my bedroom and open up my bottom drawer where I keep my treasures.

"There she is." I say out loud. My lucky coin. Mom's coin she gave me.

I grab it, look at it for a moment because I haven't held this in my hands for years.

 I slip it in my pocket and head for the door.

I go to the parking garage, place my key in my ignition and head to the house. I need to be there. I'm numb and feel like I'm dreaming.

What am I driving up to, walking into?

My hands hold the steering wheel tightly, knuckles white, and for the first time since grammar school, I begin to pray.

"Dear Lord, please, I beg of you, please let her be ok. Please, I pray that you are listening. I am so sorry I haven't talked to you. I suck so bad at this. I'm sorry. Please Lord, forgive me for swearing. Just hear me out. I will do anything to make her ok. I know I think terrible thoughts sometimes of her and I know I haven't been the best human, but please, I beg you, PLEASE! Don't let her go. Please, Lord, hear my prayer! Hear me!" I feverishly search for the right words to say, the right feelings to feel.

Luckily, I hit every green light between my apartment and the house I grew up in and make it there in record time. *Maybe God is listening*, I think to myself.

I barely throw the car in park, as I run up the driveway to the door, stop.

I take a breath in and exhale, grab the door handle to open it when Hayden opens it for me.

"Hayden," I say as our eyes meet.

He grabs me in his arms and my head rests on his chest and he holds me tightly for a long moment.

"Where is she?" I ask while still holding him because I don't want to let go.

He pulls back and bends his head to me, looking into my eyes.

"Sam. Sam, look at me."

I look at him, feeling his arms now at my waist.

"Sam, listen to what I have to say..."

He has my full attention.

He pauses. "Your mother has taken a turn for the worse. The pneumonia is filling her lungs. The onset of it has turned rapid and severe. Sam, she needs you and your dad to be strong right now."

"What?" I am trying hard to digest his words but all I can hear are bits and pieces. Severe. Pneumonia, but trying to piece everything together.

"How did this happen? She was just talking to me yesterday, telling me she wanted to have her friends over?"

"Sam, I can't tell you why nor can I tell you if she will get better. I *can* tell you that your mother told me that she wanted to be home, no matter how she feels. She and I went over a plan at the hospital the day she was discharged, and she was adamant that she wanted to be home, whether she became worse or got better. And, as her physician and as someone who cares, we must respect her wishes."

I go to say something, mouth partially open, ready to battle what he's saying, but I stop.

I need to see her first; I need to see my mother.

"I understand, Hayden. I do. Where is she?" I let go of our embrace and walked into my parents' home, not knowing where she was.

Dad was walking down the stairs and heard me.

"Sammy, she is up in our room," He comes closer to me, "But, Sammy, before you go up, you have to understand that your mom is not well. Sam, Dr. Bryant has called hospice and they should be here shortly. She needs us, baby girl. She needs us to be there for her."

We look at each other, both of us quiet, not knowing what to say.

So, he finishes.

"Your mother has taken care of us for the best part of our lives. She has been our strength. Now, we need to do our part and be hers."

His eyes fill up with tears and his voice cracks. He needs me to be there for them both.

"Daddy," I held onto both his hands, "Yes, Hayden briefed me. Dad. We got this." I say and head to her room.

As I approach her room, walking down the hallway to their room, I can hear mother's favorite album playing from her old record player she loves, *All the Things You Are* by Ella Fitzgerald, one of her and dad's favorite songs and hearing this makes this so real.

I walk to the door wide open and stop to bend my head in fear of both waking her and fear of what I am about to see.

"She isn't sleeping, Sam. The last time she woke up and responded to me was 11 last night. It's been almost 5 hours since she has been conscious. But, Dr. Bryant said she could be in and out. Her body is taking over her mind." Dad says to me as he walks past me where I am standing in the doorway to the room.

I take another step into their room.

On her nightstand, I see a glass of water, on the floor her house slippers are placed perfectly along the side of the bed. I wonder if dad put them there, hoping her feet would find them, once again.

As I draw closer, she is lying on her side of the bed. She has always slept on that side since I was a little girl, and I was certain it was because it was closest to her other room she kept locked. And on the other side, dad's side, it is perfectly made. I look to where she's laying and notice that someone must have brought up dad's recliner and place it near her side so that he can sit with her.

Dad notices me looking at the chair, "Dr. Bryant brought it up for me. He insisted I be comfortable and as close to your mom as I could."

I look up at the doorway where Hayden is standing and mouth to him, "Thank you."

He closes his eyes and nods his head; just another way of letting me know he cares.

I walk over to my mother.

Her hands are resting alongside her waist side near her hips, I notice on her left hand her wedding band on and in her other hand, a rosary and I recognize it; it's a family heirloom on her mother's side. The rosary has been on her dresser for as long as I can remember.

I sit in dad's chair and take her hand in mine, she feels so frail, and her hands are ice cold. I lean forward and in a low voice I say, "Mother? Can you hear me? Squeeze my hand if you can hear me."

I wait for seconds hoping for just a little squeeze, look from her closed eyes to my hand holding hers hoping for a squeeze.

Nothing.

I can feel Hayden and Dad's eyes on me; I look up at them and shrug my shoulders. Dad nods in understanding. He can feel my pain, my desperate desire to connect with her.

Hayden pipes up.

"Mr. Jenkins, do you want to join me in the kitchen? It's almost 5am and I'm thinking you must be hungry. I'll make us something to eat, Samantha and I got some breakfast items when we went shopping. Eleanor needs us strong."

Dad is leaning against the wall, looking exhausted. I agree he needs to sit and eat because right now he looks so lost. As he is staring at Mother I realize he didn't hear a word Hayden had said. In my heart, I think he's still waiting for the squeeze as much as I am.

"Daddy?" He hears me and he looks at me.

"Yeah, sweetheart?" he responds, raising his eyebrows oblivious to us speaking.

"Dad, Hayden is going to the kitchen to make us some breakfast. Why don't you join him and take some time to rest. I'm here now and can sit with my mother."

I cup her hand now with both of mine, trying to bring some warmth to her.

"Ok, yes," he looks over to Hayden, "sure." He comes to, snapping himself out of the gaze toward mother, "Yes. Sure, Hayden, I could use some food and a cup of coffee."

And these two men, who mean so much to me, go to eat together.

My eyes follow them out the door and I look back at my mom.

Here we are again. Just her and me. I see that in the last twelve hours I've been away, her color has changed. She is a pale color I haven't seen before. Nevertheless, she is still so beautiful. I sit up and notice her hair looks ruffled. She wouldn't want this, so I run my fingers through her hair, pushing it away from her eyes then pulling it back and very gently tucking the strands behind her ear. When I was little she did this a lot, tucked my hair behind my ears; I couldn't sit still for the life of me, and my hair would be a mess by the end of the day. So, she would always be tucking my hair and making sure I looked presentable. As I tucked, mother's body took an obvious breath that felt out of sequence to her breathing.

I stop for a minute, then pull away as though I may have hurt her; then I realize it was the opposite, she feels me.

'Mother?" I ask and she gives no response, only falls back into her breathing pattern.

I look over at her and think for a minute, then take her hand and turn it over with her palm up, carefully placing the rosary aside on her nightstand.

I take her hand and can see the lines in her palm. I trace her lines with my finger going from one end of her hand to the other side. I never noticed before how old her skin feels until now. It seems so thin, almost like it could tear at any point. I have failed this woman. She has been aging while I have been working and doing my own thing and in the meantime, I've been losing time with her. Why didn't I see that she needed me? Why haven't I noticed this? Was I so self-absorbed that I took time for granted? I'm sitting here feeling so ashamed of how I would roll my eyes when I saw her number calling me. How I would tell her I'm super busy, but would call as soon as I could, only to call too many days later. I would imitate her with Dexter, and we would crack up laughing and it wasn't because I was trying to be mean but deep down it was because I love her and there are parts of her that I love the most and would mock her. I know how that sounds, but all the things that used to annoy me as a child are now the reasons I love her the most and can't help the moments that I sound like her and would have a laugh over it.

My mind is racing in every direction to find ways that I've failed her.

"Mother, I am so sorry. Please forgive me." I say as I trace and gently rub her hand in hopes she can feel me and know I'm here.

She continues to lay there, as still as night until she makes a loud ominous sound that scares me half to death. She continues to groan in a way that sounds both painful and hard for me to hear.

I scream "MOTHER!" I wait for one second. She continues to lay still, no more sound from her, only her breathing that seems to have taken up speed.

"Samantha?" I hear Hayden running up the stairs yelling my name with Dad trailing behind him.

He bolts into the room, "Sam what is it?!" He asks.

I'm standing there frozen in shock.

"Hayden. Mother. She was in pain, I think. She didn't wake up but definitely was in pain. Hayden? What should I do?" I beg of him, pleading.

He looks at me for what seems like a long time and a calmness comes over him; he comes around, grabs his stethoscope, and kneels down beside the bed and begins to check her vitals.

I say nothing. Dad and I just watch as he heroically begins to do what he does every day at the hospital. He assesses her vitals, checks her temperature, opens her eyes and shines his light into them and as he does this, I watch how gentle he is, speaking to her as though she can hear him.

"Okay, Eleanor, I'm going to now check your heart," almost as though asking permission. As he goes through the steps that are second nature to him, he catches me watching him.

"Don't worry. This is normal for a patient in her condition," He reassures me.

We wait for him to be done and he turns to us both as dad is beside me with his arms around me.

"Ok, Mr. Jenkins. I suggest we place her on morphine. We want her to be as comfortable as possible. As we near the end of life, it can be a challenge and that's why with morphine we can achieve pain relief for her. We don't want Eleanor to suffer any more than she has to. Mr. Jenkins, this is why we had a discussion at the hospital with her regarding end-of-life treatments. So, we can give Eleanor a voice for when or if she is nearing the end."

"Daddy?" I look to my father. "Wait. You guys discussed this? Without me?"

Dad extends his hand and says very matter-of-factly, "Samantha, these are conversations we have had for years. What we want when we go, how we go, and if I or your mother goes first. This, Samantha, is your mother's choice. Hayden called hospice and planned for them to visit. This is your mother's choice."

I say nothing. I am taking this in. My mother, still leading this family.

I look at her, bend down to her face and kiss her cheek and look straight at Hayden.

"I don't want her in pain. Do exactly what she has asked of you. I know you will take care of her."

Hayden walks over to me and places his hand on my right cheek.

"Thank you."

I head downstairs to take a breath and rest; this was a lot to digest, to accept.

I flop onto the couch and my heart sinks. I need to escape and be alone here in my home, the rooms I grew up in. In that moment I realize that mother wants to be home not so she can be comfortable, but so we will be.

"Damn," I say to myself.

I pull my knees up to my chest, grab them, and feel the heat from the fireplace, knowing mother is upstairs and Hayden is giving her morphine. This is a feeling I can't describe, a confidence that she is safe with him.

I lay my head back, looking up at the chandelier; mother loves this light. She had it shipped in from France when I was young, and it was always a hot topic for friends who visited.

I am feeling the heaviness of the day hit me hard.

Tears are rolling down both sides of my face and into my hair; now that they're falling they're coming out nonstop.

"There was so much I wanted to tell you, so much I wanted to share. There is so much I need to be for you," I say aloud.

I close my eyes trying to stop the tears but they're not stoppable. I need to get a hold of myself, to rest myself and my soul. But the loss of my mother is unbearable, and the tears just need to fall.

I love my mother and I need her. I need her to know this. I shake my head trying to release and rid these feelings.

I take a deep breath and inhale to calm myself down. I slowly let it out, feeling the air leaving my whole body. I feel my muscles begin to relax, feeling calmer and before I know it, I quietly fall asleep.

* * * * * * * * *
*

I am not sure how long I've been sleeping but I feel a blanket being placed over my body. I can't wake up, my eyes struggle to open.

"Thank you," I say without knowing who is placing my mother's lap blanket on me.

Well, not until I felt lips press on my forehead and the smell of Hayden pass by my nose.

"Hey," I say, half groggy. I force my eyes open as he sits beside me and places his hand on my knee.

"Hey yourself, sleepy girl," he says with a bit of a smile.

"How is she?' I sit up and rub out the sleepiness in my eyes, taking the elastic out of my bun that's all over the place.

"She is on morphine now. Your dad and I stayed with her for a couple of hours, but I encouraged your dad to get some sleep and he went down, I believe, in your room?"

I nod my head yes and lean back against the couch, "How long have I been out?"

"I think maybe four hours because it's a little past 9. Hospice is here with her now."

Oh gosh I need to get up; I need to be with her. I can't be laying around leaving my mother's care and comfort up to others.

I have to be with her.

"Hold on, pretty lady. I cooked you breakfast; let's grab a bite then we can go up. She is good right now. It's important that you eat."

He takes my hand and without waiting for an answer he tugs me into the kitchen where he has breakfast waiting on the counter, "How do you take your coffee?" he asks, pouring me a cup.

"Well done," I wink at him, "I like mine black."

"Coming right up," Hayden places my coffee in front of me on the kitchen island where I am sitting on a bar stool.

I say, "Dr. Bryant, I have one for you. When does an attorney make coffee?"

I see the wheels turning in Hayden's head; he is really thinking about this. I laugh at his desire to know the answer.

'Wait," he says, "Don't tell me. I think I know this!"

He thinks.

"Okay. When?" he gives in.

"On sufficient grounds," I say proudly and see his face grimace, "Yeah, that was bad," I laugh teasingly.

He comes around the island and sits by me delivering my breakfast he warmed up in the microwave.

"I already ate with your dad, but we saved you some," he says.

"Thank you, Hayden," this man is amazing. So kind, so thoughtful, and not to mention he smells amazing even after a long night.

"So, Jenkins, this is the first time we wake up in the same house?" He asks and winks at me.

"Um, yeah I guess it is. Except, I look like a wreck, and you look," I stop and read his eyes. Should I continue? Does he want me to? So, I continue and repeat "You look handsome."

He leans his head toward me as I shove a bite in my mouth and kisses me on the lips with a mouthful of eggs.

"Oops, I'm so sorry," he says.

I swallow my food and give him a quick kiss and say, "Don't be."

I love our banter. But really, where can this go? With his schedule and mine, and now with mother, I just don't see this going anywhere, so I get my wits about me and change the subject.

"Do you think my mom will get better?" I ask.

"Well, Sam, everything in me wants to lie to you on this. But your mother's body is tired. She has retired due to her health, and I think it's important we understand that she may not make it and if she does, I can tell you, she may not want to go back to the hospital."

I knew this. I knew this before I even asked but I appreciate and value his honesty.

I sit for a brief moment thinking about his words as I take a sip of my coffee.

"She has lived well. You know, the other day I was thinking about when I was little. Dad and I used to go to the school where he teaches; he spent so much time with me. My mother and I, our relationship was different. Her time with me was different but meant just as much now that I look back. I know we grew up well to do and all, but I can honestly say that my mother would carefully give me lessons without me realizing. Once we were driving to school and I must have been all of eight years old. Here she was driving me to the best private school around and she took the long way around to get there. Looking back now, I get why. She purposely drove me through the roughest streets of New York City, where there were rows of tents for the homeless. As we would pass by, she would tell me that these families looked like us. That these people were veterans that fought for our country, that these children were the children of moms and dads who work but cannot afford a place to live so they choose food instead of shelter for their children. That these people are a test of our kindness, and we should always give to help others so that we never lose ourselves in what we have been blessed with. I remember seeing these tents, the people with carts looking awful. She took this route every single day and now I see it was because she didn't want me to lose my sense of compassion. She showed her love through lessons and even though those lessons felt harsh, she showed me every day what an incredibly strong woman she was. Maybe that's why sometimes I feel like I am not strong, because I could never be half as strong as she is."

I catch myself, "I'm so sorry. I'm rambling."

"Don't be," He pauses. "You know, Sam, she can hear you. If you talk to her now she would be able to hear you. Maybe she needs to hear your heart." He walks over to me and places his arms around me and holds me. I lean my head on his chest.

Can she hear me? I think to myself.

I look up at him and say, "I'm going to spend the morning with her. Why don't you clean up and come back later. With hospice here, I think you can duck out and take care of things you need to?"

"If you don't mind. I need to swing over to the hospital; I have a change of clothes there and I need a shower. I need to update her file and meet with Dr. Piper, but I will be back after lunch, ok?"

"Of course! You have done so much already," I say to him and mean it.

"Ok, so I will call you before I head back in case you want me to pick something up?" He asks.

"Sounds good, Hayden, thank you."

I watch him leave, giving me time to be with my mother, time I know I will remember for the rest of my life.

*   *   *   *   *

    *   *   *   *

I wash my hands, throw the towel on the counter, and make myself another cup of coffee then head upstairs.

I peek in on dad who is fast asleep in my old bedroom; I walk over to him and pull the covers up to his shoulders where he can be warmer, then I stand over him watching him sleep.

My sweet daddy, a good man.

A man of honor.

A man of great love.

A man who loves his girls so much; we are definitely his ladies. I smile at him.

He has done a wonderful job raising me.

I can see he likes Hayden; I am certain he would love for me to be with someone like him.

Maybe eventually I will find someone like my father, but only when I'm ready. Life is hectic right now and I have my own things that I need to figure out. Until then, my dad will be the one man I'll focus on.

His heart is breaking right now and it's important for me to be there for him, like he has always been there for me.

He's aging, I see this now. I have wasted way too much time on myself, and I need to focus on them.

I walk out of my old bedroom and into my parents' room, across the hallway.

I see a nurse and what looks to be her aide, washing mother's legs and cleaning her up. I stand back and watch them.

I am not sure what my mother would think of this if she realized another person was bathing her. I'm not sure if she would be embarrassed or if she would feel pampered and important. Either way, she deserves to be clean, to feel good, because lying in her bed, she would definitely want to look her best.

They see that I am in the room, and they wrap up what they are doing.

"We want you to have time with your mother, so we are going to leave you with her, ma'am. Dr. Bryant will be here this afternoon, but we are here until then. Could we go to the kitchen for coffee?" The nurse asks me.

"Oh, yes, of course," I assure her. "Please help yourself to anything. It may be a rough couple of days so please help yourself and if you need anything, tell me and I will get it."

She was very appreciative and thanked me.

I was aware of hospice before now; I had worked with their trust accounts to know and be familiar with why they are there and for how long.

I know the end is coming.

I sit with my mother for over an hour staring at her, trying to memorize every contour of her face, trying to focus on every inch of her that I never want to forget. I am trying to shove years into this moment so that I will never forget her.

Her hands. I stare down at her hands for the longest time because I never want to forget these hands, or how much my hands look like hers. So many times, as a little girl, I would watch her hands bake cakes, hold books reading to me and even take her hands, licking her thumb, and then wiping stuff off my face.

I grab my phone, lift her hand up and snuggle my hand under hers, as though we are holding hands and I snap a picture.

I never want to forget. One day, I say to myself, I will paint this, I will paint our hands together. I make a mental note of this moment and to not ever forget it.

I notice dad's empty spot next to hers and get up and lay carefully beside her. I lay my head on her shoulder and hold her hand.

"I never thought the day would come that I would be so close to losing you. My whole life I lived under your spell. You were the woman, the mom who could do anything. You were one of the only moms who always had her daughter's back. I know, Mom, you were tough on me and believe me," I laugh to myself, "believe me. I get this from you, but every single day of my life, I always knew you loved me."

I have tears rolling from my eyes as I continue pouring my heart out to the only woman who has ever loved me and the only woman I call mom.

"Please mom forgive me for not visiting. Not calling. Damn it, for not doing what I should have and that is taking care of you. Please mom, I am so sorry. "

I remember I have my coin with me; I can almost hear her years ago when she bought this for me. "We are women of strength and courage and never forget this." I reach into my pocket with my right hand to find the coin.

I look at it, kiss it, and then place it in the middle of her hand pressed between our palms.

"I need your strength right now. I need you right now. I need you to know how much I love you," I place my head on her shoulder, my tears soaking the shirt she is wearing.

"Mom, I pray that I've made you proud."

I lay there for a while with Ella Fitzgerald playing in the background.

At this moment, I realize this is the closest I have ever been with her, the longest we've laid together. This, regardless of mother being asleep, may very well be the most beautiful time I have had with her.

"I love you, mom," I whisper and close my eyes.

Without skipping a beat, I feel a twitch in her hand that I'm holding.

Then, my hand feels like it's being squeezed, and I can feel the coin pressing more firmly against mine. I look down at my hand and realize she's squeezing my hand.

I look back up at her, and her eyes are trying to open, they flutter as she struggles to open them.

"Mom?"

Her lips are moving, and no sound is coming out of them. I sit cross-legged next to her with both hands on her face.

"Mother? Can you hear me?" I plead for an answer.

"Mother!" I raise my voice.

'Sammy," She mumbles and repeats, "Sam."

"Yes, mother. Yes I can hear you. I am here, mother!" I am beside myself.

"I love you, too. I.." She is trying so hard to talk to me and I am doing everything I can to listen while rubbing her hands, her face, her hair, anything I can do to keep her talking.

"I am so proud of you, my girl," she says, and her lips curl up at the end almost to smile at me.

I need this. She knows I need this. I wrap my arms around her arm and pull myself as close as I can to her, snuggle next to her so she can feel me. I cannot get close enough. It was almost like I need my soul as close to her as it can possibly be at this moment.

I've never felt true love before and in this moment, I feel a true force between us. It feels full, unconditional, and plain good. My whole life, she was the last to eat, the last to shower, the last to go to bed. Always placing us first before herself. I took for granted that she would be the last to leave this earth, and in any way I can,

I want to hold her as she becomes the first to leave us. I want her to leave feeling loved, needed, and appreciated.

I want her to leave feeling like her job was well done, that she was a great mom.

I had spent every day of my life behind this amazing woman wanting to be like her, wanting to be everything she ever wanted in a daughter. Deep down, I knew. I knew she would always wear shoes I could never fill.

But in this moment, a moment I pray I will never forget, there is a beauty, a strength in us both. Her hand in mine, lying next to her. A power deep down in my soul that I know is from her.

And in that moment I feel, finally, I can and will spend the rest of my life being me and that I am someone she will always be proud of. Even if it's from her seat in Heaven.

"I love you, mama," I whisper.

<u>Final Chapter</u>

I feel everyone's eyes on me at the house after the funeral as I run around filling chip bowls and refreshing the punch, filling my time with useless tasks to avoid people.

"Ms. Jenkins, I am so sorry about your mother. I knew her from the shelter," This elderly lady extends her hand to mine, holding my hands in hers, "She was a good woman. Always wanting to help us. If you can, please come down to the shelter. We would love to introduce you to the team. She meant a lot to them."

"I would love that. Yes, I will come by," and I thank her for coming.

It's unfamiliar faces with their own stories about her. Over and over. I look across the room at dad; he's talking to Mr. Jalbert. He saw him at the church and nudged me showing me that he had come. It made us smile at one another. It was comforting to see him there. I know for dad it meant more than he could explain, a piece of their history lives in this man's heart and that little empty table in the corner.

I see them embrace one another across the room and dad is grinning while Mr. Jalbert talks away, Most likely revisiting those days at the diner. Whatever it is, dad looks younger as he's smiling.

I hope in moments like this, he finds her again.

"Samantha?" I'm startled to hear my name and turn to see Dexter.

"Samantha, how are you doing?" He takes both my hands, "I have been so worried about you. How are you?"

I grab hold of him and hug him, "Dexter, thank you. Honestly, I am good. Holding strong. It has been a rough two weeks. But…" I inhale and exhale, "But right now I am focusing on Dad and what this looks like for him." I look at him talking to Mr. Jalbert and

Dexter looks over at him, "I want to make sure he is doing ok. I mean, I know it won't be ok, but he relied on her for so much, Dex. I am afraid I am going to need to move back home and be his rock. I am really not sure he knows what lies ahead."

Dexter looks at me and grins.

"You may be surprised, Sam. Your father was trained by the best. Your mother ran a tight ship. You are going to be alright and so will he. But I am confident someone else won't be as ok..." and he nods over to Hayden who is sitting on the sofa with a plate of food talking to the Southern nurse, Charlene. She is flipping her hair to the other side sitting as close to him as possible.

Hayden can feel our stare and looks over at us with a please-help-me look.

Dexter continues.

"He may need you to save him," and giggles.

'He's fine," I say to Dexter and smile.

'Well, he can either be fine with you or he can be fine with the nurse. You decide," and he pushes me toward them. I entertain Dexter's suggestion and walk over to them.

"Ms. Jenkins. How are y'all doing?" Charlene asks with genuine concern, "We have been praying for you and your daddy."

"Thank you Charlene. It means a lot that you came. We appreciate all you've done. My father and I wondered if we could take all the flowers we received back to the hospital. We have so many and thought maybe some of the patients could use a bit of cheering up?"

"Oh, honey. That would be so kind of you!!" She says in a high-pitched voice.

Just then I notice Gary from the office walking by, shoving snacks in his mouth, dressed in a frumpy suit as short as he is.

"Hey Gary! Over here," Gary walks over to us, "Gary, this is Charlene, mother's nurse. Charlene, this is Gary from the firm. He is one of our paralegals."

Charlene butts in, "Oh, Gary! Thank you so much for your contribution to the fundraiser. It was so kind of y'all."

I look over at Dexter and he is nearly in hysterics; Gary for his part is a little overwhelmed by Charlene's excitement, "Oh, yeah, thanks."

I look down at Hayden sitting on the couch and give him a wink.

"Hey Gary, the flowers out front from mother's funeral, we want to donate to the hospital and wondered if you can help me and place them in Charlene's car?" I suggest and without a beat Charlene says apologetically, "Oh, I'm so sorry, Ms. Jenkins, but I took a cab here today. I use public transportation. I don't have a car to bring those flowers to the hospital."

I recover quickly and ask, "Well, Gary, would it be okay if we put them in your car and have Charlene join you and bring them to the patients?"

"Um, ok. Yeah, sure," he responds in a monotone voice.

"Wonderful!" Charlene says and grabs her purse then heads to the door.

Dexter walks over to us and says, "There you go, Gare Bear. Go help a lady."

Gary walks out behind Charlene, shuffling his feet along the way.

Dexter flashes me a smile and starts humming from a musical, "Matchmaker, matchmaker, make me a match," and walks away and starts a conversation with a couple of attorneys from the office.

Hayden looks at me and mouths, "Thank you."

I giggle, "Yeah, no problem. I figured you needed saving."

"Yeah, it was quickly escalating to that, yes," he reaches over and grabs my hand, "How are you doing, Jenkins?"

I can feel my heart skip a beat. I love it when he calls me that.

I look at him and say "Good. I am doing well. Thank you, Hayden, for taking such great care of my parents and my mother for the last two weeks. I will never know how to repay you…"

"Stop. You already have." and he bends his head and kisses me on the cheek with one hand on my other cheek.

I tilt my head in the direction of his kiss and can feel our heads pause against one another and for a moment I can feel my body heat up and my lips wanting to find his; I shoot to my feet.

"Hayden, don't be a stranger. You do know you can come by anytime?"

He clears his throat and responds with, "I knew that weeks ago and plan on never stopping my visits. Jenkins, there is something about you that I can't shake. Trust me, I won't be a stranger. You may find yourself seeing me far more often than you think," and he gives my hand a squeeze and walks over to my father and shakes his hand.

I watch them interact.

My father hugs him, then holds Hayden's arm and shakes his other hand. I can see my father trying to keep it together and then they both look my way as I watch them.

These two men. My father who I absolutely love. The man that built me. The man that became the model of the man I will one day want to marry.

And then there was Hayden. The man that I feel I have known forever. The man that carries my heart into a space I have never experienced. A man that I am falling in love with.

I smile toward them and give them a little wave.

The November chill fills the air and I get up and head up to my parent's room to find a mother's sweater I can wear.

Heading to their room, I can still smell my mother's perfume, the one she always wore. Her smell. I walk into her room and open her closet and see an abundance of sweaters, all color coded. It brings a smile to my face. She was always so organized, a trait I wish I inherited from her. I grabbed her coral sweater that she loved wearing to the ocean. I look in her mirror and pull it on, wrapping it around myself snugly, like a hug from her. I wrap my arms around my waist and close my eyes, trying so hard to feel her.

I look at the door in the mirror, her little room she kept locked. That room was always her private space. I noticed her purse in the corner and remembered my ring attached to a key ring she had in her purse. On that key ring, I remember it in the hospital seeing a key on it.

I walk over and rummage through the purse pulling out the key with my little ring I had as a child.

"Mom, what in the world made you want to keep this little ring?" I ask aloud.

I walk over to the door that was locked and slowly place the single key in the keyhole hoping it fits and I turn the knob and feel a click. It unlocks.

"Samantha?" I hear my father's voice.

"Oh, dad. Hi. I'm sorry. I found this key and I…" I quickly say.

"Samantha. It's ok." He walks over and stands in front of me.

"I know you've been curious your whole life about this room, and I know your mother would one day want you to go into it. And I am not sure if this is that time or not, but…" He says.

"Dad?" I ask, watching him.

"Samantha…" and he brings me to the bed and sits me down.

"Samantha, your mother loved you like no other. Every single day of your life she would tell me how much she loved you and how you were everything she wished she could be. Everyday Samantha. Every day, she would come into this room. This room meant a lot to her, Samantha. And I knew this day was going to come but I didn't think it would be this soon."

Tears begin to fall from his face.

"Dad, I am so confused, what are you.."

He cuts me off, grabs my hand, and walks me over to the door to the room.

He slowly opens it and the sunlight across the room is beaming in our eyes. The room is dusty but filled with light. I smell a familiar smell, a comforting smell. He walks me over to an extra-large vintage storage trunk.

He looks at me and says.

"Samantha, your mother loved you. She was so proud of you and everything you accomplished. She was your biggest fan and couldn't ever stop talking about how gifted you are."

I am so confused, I don't know what to say. Gifted? A gifted attorney who never found time to visit. A gifted attorney who avoided coming home for the sake of not disappointing her parents.

My father bends down and unlatches the trunk.

He stands up slightly and grabs ahold of both sides of the cover and gives it a tug to open.

He looks up at me and says, "Sam. Please, before I open this, know how much she loved you." and he opens up the vintage trunk exposing a row of packed canvas neatly packed in the trunk.

I couldn't see what they were except there were about a dozen of them.

He stands up and looks at me, reaches down and slides out the first one.

It's a painting. I know this painting.

I looked at it confused, staring at its portrait of the New York city skyline.

I knew this painting because it was mine from ten years ago when I was a student in law school; only a couple of years ago I placed it for sale at the gallery.

"Dad? This is mine," I feel my face grow red; I feel the hairs on my arms rising to attention.

"Yes, Samantha, I know this, and your mother knew this. She was your biggest fan. She loved your work and every chance she could, she would go to the gallery and see your paintings or sketches."

I looked at my father, "She knew?"

"Yes, Sam, she did. She knew and was in love with your talent," he shares.

"But why didn't she say anything? Why didn't she tell me?" I whisper.

And he says carefully, but clearly, "The same reason you didn't tell her, sweetheart."

He grabs my hand and brings me over to an area where there is a large piece of muslin cloth covering something large.

"Samantha, give me a hand and grab and end," asking me to uncover whatever it was that was underneath.

Together we pull the cloth back, kicking dust in the air making us both cough and choke.

I notice it's a very large life size canvas with a chair and some paints on the floor in front of it. I walk around in front of it.

My heart sinks, my jaw drops.

I cannot believe what I'm looking at.

"Who…What…" I am shaking my head and looking at my father, "Who painted this?"

There in front of me is an almost finished painting of a little girl standing in front of a large oval mirror; the little girl is in an oversized dress with large shoes that swallow the size of her feet. She's in the mirror looking at herself with one little hand near her lips, applying it to her own itty-bitty mouth. In the corner of the painting, I see the initials E.J. Eleanor Jenkins. My mother.

This little girl… is… me.

"Dad," I feel my eyes filling with tears; I need to sit down and place myself carefully in the chair in front of the piece.

"Dad… she painted this," I can barely speak.

"Yes, honey. Your mother was a beautiful artist. She has been painting since she was little. It was a beautiful gift her parents stole from her. It was a beautiful gift she was raised to be embarrassed of. It was a beautiful gift that filled her soul, and she knew this gift was a gift you inherited."

I look up at dad and say, "She knew. She knew I painted. She knew all these years. All these years I've been hiding, afraid she wouldn't be happy about it. All those years, she knew."

"She did. But if you knew that she knew, then you would also know she was shamed by her parents for this gift. That you would see it as a curse to your successes just like her parents taught her to believe. She wanted you to be more than your gift. She wanted you to be more than she ever could be. In her heart, she loved that you painted but couldn't face it herself. She never looked back after her parents forbade her to paint. Then when you were painting as a child, it pulled a spark out of her that I hadn't seen in years. She became alive when seeing your artwork."

"Dad, I'm so sorry. I'm so sorry for keeping this from you both. I could have done more." and I began to cry.

He comes to my side, kneels down, and takes my face in his hands.

"Sweetheart, the best part of you, the person only you see in the mirror. The person you are each night you go to bed, that's the best part of your mother. You are the most beautiful part of the woman I married. You are as beautiful, gifted, and stubborn," we both smile, "as your mother but every best part of you is my favorite part of her. She loved you, Sammy. She loved all of you."

"Dad…" I hang onto his neck holding and hugging him.

Dad takes my hands and says words that will cling to my soul for the rest of my life and the rest of the decisions I will ever make.

"Sammy, when that man downstairs looks at you. When Hayden looks at you, he looks at you the same way I used to look at your mother. He is in love with you. Your mother would want this for you. Every time you look in the mirror, my sweet girl, every time you miss your mother, you go look in the mirror and you will see your mother looking right back at you. Telling you to go for it.

I look at my dad for a moment and then back at the painting.

I slowly raise my hand to touch this little girl in the painting, my mother's painting.

I am about to go for it.

I am about to let myself fall deeply, madly, ridiculously, in love with Hayden Bryant.

Acknowledgments

With every inch of my heart and soul, I cannot thank those who believed in me and my love for writing.

Special thanks to Melissa & Kristin who believed I could and I did.

To my beautiful husband, Danny, who is the love of my life and my incredible children; thank you for being my greatest love.

To my editor, Shannon, who just believed. Who just knew. And who had open arms right from the beginning.

To my mom and my sisters. Thank you for loving me unconditionally. My heart cannot thank you for loving me through my triumphs and my failures.

Buffy Dumont is a serial entrepreneur who grew up and lives in the small town of Monmouth, Maine with her husband. Together they raised five children and now live vicariously through the eyes of their grandchildren. She owns and operates Integrity Homes Real Estate with the same kind of love she has for writing. She and her husband love traveling to Aruba, sitting on their back deck in Maine and spending Sundays with their children for Family Dinner.

Since the early age of 10 she has poured her heart into journals becoming a fascinating and a safe way to express feelings.

S.E. Jenkins series will carry you through the hearts of The Jenkins Family while helping you realize the best kinds of memories go straight to your heart and live beautifully there forever.

Made in the USA
Coppell, TX
01 May 2023